Evan

A CHRISTMAS NOVEL

ANGEL INSTITUTE
BOOK SIX

ERICA PENROD

ANGEL INSTITUTE LLC

Copyright © 2024 by Erica Penrod

All rights reserved.

No part of this book may be reproduced in any form or by any electronic or mechanical means, including information storage and retrieval systems, without written permission from the author, except for the use of brief quotations in a book review.

Dear Reader,

We're so delighted you're here! Welcome to Angel Institute, where romance, Christmas magic, and angels-in-training come together to share the Spirit of Christmas right in the heart of Benton Falls.

This series draws inspiration from some of the most beloved Christmas classics, including—but certainly not limited to—*It's a Wonderful Life*, *A Christmas Carol*, *White Christmas*, and, of course, the greatest story ever told—the birth of our Savior, Jesus Christ, when angels proclaimed tidings of great joy.

As you journey through these stories, we hope you'll feel the wonder of the season, the warmth of love for your family and sweetheart, and, most importantly, the deep love God has for you.

Heaven is always mindful of you, dear friend. There are angels all around you, cheering you on and working for your good. Our prayer is that as you read, you'll

DEAR READER,

recognize their presence, feel their support, and rejoice with them this Christmas.
 Merry Christmas!
 Lucy & Erica

Prologue

BETTY

I slide into my seat at the polished wooden desk, the celestial symbols etched into its surface seeming to dance before my eyes. I lean over to Gladys, my fellow angel-in-training, and whisper, "I'm so nervous."

"Me too," she nods and offers me a reassuring smile. Her blonde curls bounce with the gesture.

Henry, our ever-patient mentor, takes his place at the front of the room, his wings folded neatly behind him. "Alright, class, settle down," he says, his voice laced with amusement. "Today's the big day. You'll each receive your final assignment on Earth, just in time for the Christmas season."

I rub my hands together in excitement. "I love Christmas. I can't wait to spread some holiday cheer." I've been practicing my 'Ho, ho, ho!' for weeks now."

John, the gruff angel next to me, raises an eyebrow. "Betty, I thought we were supposed to be teaching about the gifts of the season, not impersonating Santa Claus."

I elbow him playfully. "Who says we can't do both? I'll have them feeling grateful for the joy of laughter in no time."

Henry chuckles, shaking his head. "I have no doubt about that, Betty."

As Henry distributes the letters, I think back to my own life, the challenges I faced and the strength I found through gratitude. When he hands me my envelope, I take a deep breath, sending up a silent prayer for guidance.

Dear Celestial Trainee,

Your final examination has arrived. This Christmas season, you are tasked with a mission of utmost importance—one that will determine your readiness to receive your wings and ascend to the honored rank of guardian angel.

You are hereby assigned to assist:

Evan Lawson, a Christmas tree farm owner

Your objective is to help this individual discover and embrace the true spirit of gratitude this Christmas. This task will require all the skills and compassion you have cultivated during your training at the Angel Institute.

Your success hinges on Evan's genuine understanding and application of this essential Christmas virtue.

A successful mission will earn you your wings and the privilege of becoming a guardian angel. However, failure to complete this task satisfactorily will result in a century-long delay before you may attempt this final test again.

May the light of Heaven guide you in this crucial endeavor.

Wishing you divine success,
The Angelic High Council

"Evan Lawson, a Christmas tree farm owner," I read again, and this time aloud, my voice softening with empathy.

Arthur leans over, his eyes filled with warmth. "Sounds like Evan could use a reminder of all the blessings in his life, even if they're not always obvious."

I nod, a determined smile spreading across my face. "And that's exactly what I'm going to give him. I'll help him see beauty in the little things, the everyday wonders that are so easy to overlook."

As we rise from our seats, ready to embark on our missions, I feel a sense of purpose settling over me. Laughter might be the best medicine, but I understand the power of gratitude on a profound level. It's what carried me through the darkest days of my past, and it's the gift I'm determined to share with Evan.

I step out into the heavenly gardens of vibrant blooms and gentle breezes. With a spring in my step and a prayer in my heart, I set off on my journey, ready to help Evan rediscover the transformative power of gratitude.

"Get ready, Evan Lawson," I murmur to myself, a smile playing at the corners of my lips, "Betty the Gratitude Guru is on her way." I chuckle at the title. "And she's got a pocketful of miracles with your name on them."

One

BETTY

The crisp December air tickles my nose as I arrive near the entrance of Evan Lawson's Christmas tree farm. I inhale deeply, savoring the invigorating scent of pine and the distant aroma of cinnamon wafting from the barn. Benton Falls truly is a picture-perfect town, especially during the holidays.

I glance down at my cable-knit sweater and fleece-lined boots, marveling at how authentic they feel. Blending in with the locals should be a breeze. With a spring in my step, I make my way towards the barn, ready to begin my first assignment as a guardian angel in training.

As I approach, I spot Evan helping a family load their chosen tree onto their pickup truck. His broad shoulders strain under the weight of the massive fir, but his smile seems forced, lacking the warmth and enthusiasm I'd expect from someone surrounded by such holiday cheer.

And that's why I'm here.

Once the family drives off, Evan turns and nearly collides with me. "Oh, I'm so sorry, ma'am. I didn't see you there. Are you looking for a tree?"

I chuckle and wave off his apology. "No worries, dear. I'm just here to enjoy the festive atmosphere. I'm Betty, by the way."

"Evan Lawson, nice to meet you." He extends a gloved hand, which I shake firmly. "Well, you've certainly come to the right place for holiday cheer." His words contend with his even tone. "Look around and let me know if you need any help."

"Thank you, Evan. I must say, your farm is absolutely stunning. You must put in a lot of hard work to keep it looking this good."

Evan shrugs, his gaze scanning the neat rows of trees. "It's a family business. Just doing my part to keep it running."

I tilt my head, sensing the weariness beneath his polite exterior. "And do you enjoy it? Running the farm, I mean."

He hesitates, as if surprised by my question. "I... well, it's a lot of responsibility. But it's what my family expects of me."

Before I can respond, a little girl with pigtails and a puffy pink coat tugs on Evan's sleeve. "Excuse me, Evan? Can you help me find a tree that's taller than my daddy?"

Evan's expression softens as he kneels to meet her eye level. "Of course, Leena. Let's see if we can find the perfect one."

EVAN

As they walk hand-in-hand towards the rows of trees, I'm encouraged by the change in Evan's demeanor. With the child's innocent request, he seems more relaxed, more engaged. Perhaps the key to unlocking his heart lies in the simple joys of childhood.

I meander through the farm, taking in the sights and sounds of families choosing their perfect trees. Laughter rings out across the hills, mixing with the gentle rustling of evergreen boughs in the breeze. Despite the chill in the air, warmth blooms in my chest. There's just something magical about Christmas on Earth.

As the day wears on, I keep an eye on Evan, observing his interactions with customers. He's unfailingly polite and helpful, but there's a stiffness to his movements, a distance in his eyes. It's as if he's going through the motions, disconnected from the surrounding joy.

When the last family drives away, Evan slumps against the barn wall, his shoulders sagging. I approach him cautiously, offering a thermos of hot cocoa. "You look like you could use a pick-me-up."

He accepts the thermos with a grateful nod. "Thanks, Betty. It's been a long day."

"I can imagine. Running a place like this must be exhausting, especially during the busy season."

Evan takes a sip of the cocoa, his brow furrowing. "It's not just the work. It's... I don't know. Sometimes I feel like I'm stuck, you know? Like there's more out there, waiting for me."

I nod, understanding dawning. "And the farm feels like an anchor holding you back."

"Exactly." He sighs, his breath clouding in the chilly air. "I know it sounds selfish. The farm is my family's legacy. I should be grateful for what I have." Concern casts a shadow across his features. "Sorry, I didn't mean to unload on you."

I place a gentle hand on his arm. "Evan, it's fine, and it's not selfish to want more from life. But maybe, just maybe, there's joy and purpose to be found right here, too. You just need to look at it with fresh eyes."

He meets my gaze, a flicker of hope in his blue eyes. "You think so?"

"I know so. And I have a feeling that the magic of Christmas might just help you see things differently."

Evan chuckles, shaking his head. "I guess I could use a little holiday magic right about now."

"Couldn't we all?" I wink, handing him a candy cane from my pocket. "Don't lose heart, Evan. The beauty of life has a way of sneaking up on you when you least expect it."

With that, I bid him goodnight and head back towards the road, my mind spinning with ideas. Helping Evan rediscover the joy in his life won't be easy, but I'm more determined than ever to succeed.

I focus on my heavenly home as Henry's words echo in my mind: "Follow your intuition, Betty. Trust in the power of compassion."

I take a deep breath, feeling the celestial energy coursing through me, and find myself back in heaven. Tomorrow, I'll return to Benton Falls with a plan. I'll find a way to connect with Evan, to show him the beauty and purpose that surrounds him.

For now, I'll let the warmth of the little girl's laughter and the twinkle of Christmas lights guide my dreams, reminding me of the Christmas spirit I'm here to protect.

Two

EVAN

I push through the door of Violet's Diner; the bell jingling above my head. It's late, and I'm dead on my feet after another long day at the Christmas tree farm. The warm air and the smell of fresh apple pie wrap around me like a hug, and my stomach rumbles.

Sliding into my usual booth, the red vinyl squeaking under me. Molly, the pretty waitress with the chestnut hair and the kind eyes, comes over with a pot of coffee. I've seen her around, heard she's a single mom, but we've never really talked beyond me placing my order.

"Hey there, Evan," she says, filling up my mug. "The usual tonight?"

I nod, stifling a yawn. "Yeah, thanks, Molly. Meatloaf, mashed potatoes, and green beans. You're a lifesaver."

She laughs, and it's a nice sound. "Just doing my job. Be back in a jiff with your food."

As she walks away, I can't resist watching her go. There's something about Molly, something warm and real that makes me feel less alone. But I shake off the thought. She's got enough on her plate without me mooning over her like some love-struck teenager.

I'm just about to take a sip of my coffee when a little boy with sandy hair and big, curious eyes comes barreling out of the back room. "Mom!" he yells, running up to Molly. "Guess what? I got an A on my spelling test."

Molly's face lights up, and she crouches down to give the kid a big hug. "That's amazing, Chad. I'm so proud of you."

Chad grins, bouncing on his toes. "Can we get ice cream to celebrate?"

Molly ruffles his hair. "Tell you what, buddy. If you sit quietly and do your homework while I finish my shift, we'll stop for ice cream on the way home. Deal?"

"Deal," Chad agrees, and then he's off like a shot, sliding into the booth across from me.

"Hi, mister," he says, sticking out his hand. "I'm Chad. What's your name?"

I can't help but grin at the kid's enthusiasm. "I'm Evan," I say, shaking his hand. "Nice to meet you, Chad."

Molly comes over, looking apologetic. "I'm so sorry, Evan. Chad, honey, let's not bother Mr. Lawson, okay?"

"He's not bothering me," I assure her. "Really, it's fine."

Chad looks up at Molly with those big, pleading eyes. "Can I sit with Mr. Evan, Mom? Please? I'll be good, I promise!"

Molly hesitates, but I give her a reassuring nod. "It's okay, Molly. I could use the company."

She smiles then, and it's like the sun coming out from behind a cloud. "If you're sure," she says. "Chad, you listen to Mr. Lawson and do your homework, okay?"

Chad nods solemnly. "I will, Mom."

As Molly goes to put in my order, Chad turns to me, his eyes wide with curiosity. "So, Mr. Evan, what do you do? Are you a cowboy?"

I chuckle at that. "No, buddy, I'm not a cowboy. I own the Christmas tree farm on the edge of town."

"Whoa!" Chad exclaims. "That's so cool! Do you have reindeer? Can I come see the trees sometime?"

I'm about to answer when Molly comes back with my meatloaf. She sets it down in front of me, and the smell alone is enough to make my mouth water.

"This looks amazing, as always."

"I'll pass the compliment on to the kitchen." Molly smiles.

"Mom's the best cook in the entire world," Chad declares proudly. "Better than Chef Billy."

Molly laughs, tweaking Chad's nose. "You're biased, kiddo. Now, let Mr. Evan eat his dinner in peace, okay?"

I wave off her concern. "Really, Molly, he's fine. In fact, I was just telling Chad he's welcome to come visit the farm sometime. If that's okay with you, of course."

Molly blinks, surprised. "Oh, that's... that's very kind of you, Evan. Are you sure it's not too much trouble?"

"Not at all," I assure her. "I could use a little holiday cheer around the place. And I bet Chad would love to see the trees, wouldn't you, buddy?"

Chad nods so hard I'm afraid he might strain something. "Yeah! Can we go tomorrow, Mom? Please?"

Molly hesitates, but there's a warmth in her eyes when she looks at me. "If you're sure it's no trouble, then okay. We can stop by after school tomorrow."

Chad lets out a whoop of joy, and I feel a grin spreading across my face. It's been a long time since I've had something to look forward to, something to make me feel like maybe, just maybe, there's more to life than just going through the motions.

As I dig into my meatloaf, listening to Chad chatter away about his day, I can't stop myself from stealing glances at Molly as she moves around the diner. There's a grace to her, a quiet strength that draws me in like a moth to a flame.

And when she catches me looking and gives me a shy smile, I feel something flutter in my chest, something I haven't felt in longer than I can remember.

Anticipation.

For the first time in a long time, I'm not dreading tomorrow. And as I finish my meal and say goodnight to Molly and Chad, I can't help but smile to myself.

Perhaps being stuck with the tree farm isn't all bad.

Three

EVAN

The sun's dipping behind the trees when I hear the crunch of tires on gravel. It's been a long day on the farm, getting everything ready for the Christmas rush, but my mind's been wandering. I can't shake the thought of Molly and Chad and hoping they'd really show up.

I look up and see Molly getting out of her car, Chad bouncing around like a puppy beside her. They're all bundled up, their cheeks pink from the cold. Molly's hair is escaping from her hat in little wisps, and it makes my heart do a funny little flip.

"Evan!" Chad yells, running over to me with a big grin. "We're here!"

I find myself grinning back. The kid's excitement is contagious. "Hey, buddy! You ready to learn all about Christmas trees?"

"Yeah!" he shouts, practically vibrating with energy.

"Mom said you were gonna show us around the farm and teach us everything!"

I glance at Molly, who's watching us with a kind smile. "I hope that's okay," she says, sounding a little unsure. "I know you're probably busy, but Chad hasn't stopped talking about the farm since last night. He couldn't wait to see it."

"Of course it's okay," I tell her, feeling a warmth spreading through my chest. "I'm happy to show you both around."

Molly's smile gets bigger, her eyes crinkling at the corners. "Well, lead the way then, Mr. Christmas Tree Expert."

I laugh, waving for them to follow me as I head towards the rows of trees. "All right, first lesson: not all Christmas trees are the same. You've got your firs, your pines, your spruces, and they've all got their own special qualities."

As we walk, I point out the different kinds of trees, showing them how to tell them apart by their needles and shape. Chad's hanging on every word, his eyes wide with wonder. Molly's asking questions, really interested and engaged, and before I know it, I'm lost in the conversation, just enjoying sharing something I've grown up doing with people who care.

We wander deeper into the farm, the rows of trees stretching out before us like a green maze. The air is cool and clean, filled with the sharp, fresh scent of pine. It's one of my favorite smells in the world, but lately, it's been tainted by the weight of responsibility, the burden of keeping this place running when all I want to do is escape.

But with Chad by my side, his small hand in mine, I start to see the farm through his eyes. The way the sunlight filters through the branches, casting patterns on the snow. The way the icicles glitter like diamonds, the way the wind whispers through the needles like a secret song.

"Wow," Chad breathes, his head craned back as he stares up at a towering Douglas fir. "That one's gotta be a million feet tall!"

I chuckle, ruffling his hair. "Not quite a million, buddy. But it is a beauty, isn't it?"

"It's the most beautiful tree I've ever seen," Chad declares, his voice filled with awe. "Can we take it home, Mom? Please?"

Molly laughs, the sound like music to my ears. "I think it might be a little too big for our living room, sweetie. But maybe Evan can help us find one that's just the right size."

I nod, feeling a sudden lump in my throat. "I'd be happy to. That's what I'm here for, after all."

But even as I say the words, I feel a pang of guilt. Because I'm not here for this. Not really. I'm here because it's what's expected of me. It's what my family needs me to do. My brother is in the military and my parents are off enjoying their overdue retirement. I'm here because I'm trapped, stuck in a life I never wanted, in a town I've always longed to leave behind.

But standing here, with Molly and Chad looking at

me like I'm something special, I feel a flicker of something I haven't felt in a long time. A sense of purpose, of belonging. Like maybe, just maybe, this isn't the worst place to end up.

We keep walking, Chad darting ahead to examine every tree, every pinecone, every footprint in the snow. His excitement is a tangible thing, a bright, bubbling energy that fills the air around us.

"Hey Evan," he calls out, his nose pressed against the trunk of a blue spruce. "What's this sticky stuff on the tree?"

"That's sap," I explain, crouching down beside him. "It's like the tree's blood. It flows through the trunk and branches, keeping the tree healthy and strong."

"Whoa," Chad breathes, his eyes wide. "That's so cool."

"You know what else is cool?" I ask, a grin tugging at the corner of my mouth. "If you touch the sap and make a wish, it might just come true. It's like Christmas magic."

Chad's face lights up, and he eagerly presses his hand against the sticky patch, closing his eyes tight. "I wish for the best Christmas ever," he whispers, his breath puffing out in a cloud of fog.

I feel my throat tighten, my eyes stinging with sudden tears. Because isn't that what we all want, in the end? A perfect Christmas, filled with laughter and love and joy? A moment of magic in a world that so often feels cold and dark and lonely?

I glance at Molly, seeing the emotion shimmering in

her own eyes. And I know, without a doubt, that she feels it too. The longing, the hope, the desperate wish for something more.

We keep walking, the moment passing as quickly as it came. But something has shifted between us, a subtle change in the air. Like a door has cracked open, just a sliver, letting in a hint of light.

As we round a corner, Chad lets out a gasp, his hand flying to his mouth. "Look!" he cries, pointing to a small clearing ahead. "It's a snowman!"

Sure enough, nestled among the trees is a perfect snowman, complete with a carrot nose and a jaunty top hat. His coal eyes sparkle in the fading light, his twig arms outstretched as if in welcome.

"I don't remember him being here," I murmur, frowning slightly. Neither Paul nor Seth, my part-time employees, mentioned anything about a snowman, and I doubt they would've taken the time. "I wonder who..."

But before I can finish the thought, Chad is off and running, his boots kicking up sprays of snow as he races towards the snowman. "Hi, Mr. Snowman!" he calls out, his voice ringing through the trees. "I'm Chad, and this is my mom, and this is Evan! We're here to find the perfect Christmas tree."

I shake my head, a laugh bubbling up in my chest. Leave it to a kid to make friends with a pile of snow.

But as I watch Chad chatter away to his new pal, I feel a sudden surge of emotion. For his innocence, his enthusiasm, his unshakable belief in the world's goodness.

I glance at Molly, seeing the same feelings reflected in her eyes.

An hour flies by, and we've covered nearly half the farm. Chad's starting to get tired, the cold more than likely seeping into his bones, but he insists on helping me carry some branches back to the barn for wreath-making.

"You're a natural, buddy," I tell him, messing up his hair as he carefully lays out the branches on the workbench. "Maybe you should come work for me when you're older."

Chad beams up at me, his face glowing with pride. "Really? You think I could be a Christmas tree farmer like you?"

"Absolutely," I say, my heart swelling with affection for this little kid I barely even know. "You're a natural."

Chad's smile nearly splits his face in two. "Awesome."

Molly's watching us, her eyes misty. "We should probably get going, sweetie. It's getting late, and I need to get some food in you before you turn into a hangry little monster."

"Aw, Mom!" Chad whines, sticking out his bottom lip. "Can't we stay a little longer?"

"Nope, sorry kiddo. These growling tummies wait for no man."

Chad sighs dramatically before turning to me with hopeful eyes. "Hey Evan, do you wanna come eat dinner with us? Mom makes the best spaghetti and meatballs in the whole world."

I glance at Molly, not wanting to impose, but she's smiling at me, her head tilted in invitation. "You're more than welcome to join us, Evan. It's the least we can do after you've been so kind to us today."

I feel a grin spreading across my face, a giddy sort of excitement bubbling up inside me. "I'd love to," I say, trying to play it cool. "As long as you're sure it's no trouble."

"No trouble at all," Molly assures me, her eyes warm. "Can you come in about 30 minutes?"

"Thirty minutes is perfect," I say nodding, mentally calculating how long it'll take me to clean up and look presentable. "Can I get your address?"

I hand Molly my phone. She removes her gloves, quickly types, then hands back the device.

"Thanks." I put the phone in my pocket. "I'll see you then."

"Yay!" Chad cheers, pumping his fist in the air. "Spaghetti night with Evan."

Molly laughs, herding Chad towards the car. "Come on, you little goofball. Let's let Evan finish up his work so he can come eat with us."

They wave goodbye as they drive off, Chad's face pressed against the window, his breath fogging up the glass. I wave back, feeling lighter than I have in years.

As I head back to the barn to tidy up, I can't wipe the smile off my face.

I've got a dinner date with a beautiful woman and a great kid. Okay, so maybe not a dinner date, but it's the closest thing to a romantic outing I've been on in a while.

And I can't wait to see where it leads.

Four

BETTY

I peer through the frost-dusted window of Molly's cozy bungalow, my celestial senses attuned to the warm, joyful energy emanating from within. The impromptu dinner party is in full swing, the air filled with laughter, the clinking of glasses, and the savory aroma of a lovingly prepared meal. The tree Molly and Chad picked out earlier is propped in the corner.

At the center of it all is Evan. His handsome face lit up with a genuine smile as he listens intently to one of Chad's animated stories. Molly sits beside him, her eyes sparkling with warmth and with a hint of something deeper, a budding connection that makes my angelic heart flutter with hope. I'm drawn inside to be closer to the scene playing out before me.

"And then, Mr. Whiskers jumped so high, he got stuck on top of the bookshelf," Chad exclaims, his little hands waving expressively. "It took forever to get him down."

Evan chuckles, reaching out to ruffle the boy's sandy hair. "Sounds like quite the adventurous cat you've got there, buddy."

Thankfully, there's no sign of Mr. Whiskers. A year in heaven and I'm still not comfortable with the whole communicating with animals' thing. Other angels in training say the power can be helpful, but I'd prefer to complete this assignment without the aid of a talking cat.

Molly shakes her head, a fond smile playing at her lips. "That's nothing compared to what he did last Christmas. He managed to knock over the entire tree."

"Oh, no!" Evan gasps, his eyes widening in surprise. "Not the Christmas tree."

"Yep," Molly sighs, her tone dripping with good-natured exasperation. "Ornaments everywhere, tinsel strewn about like a glittery tornado had blown through the living room. It was a sight to behold."

Evan grins, a mischievous twinkle in his eye. "Well, if it happens again this year, you know who to call. I've got connections in the Christmas tree world. We'll make sure you have the most beautiful replacement tree in all of Benton Falls."

Molly laughs, her cheeks flushing a pretty pink. "You already brought us a tree, but I'll keep that in mind. Hopefully, Mr. Whiskers has learned his lesson, but it's good to know we have a backup plan."

As I watch their easy banter, the way they gravitate towards each other with a natural, effortless chemistry, I feel a swell of hope rising in my chest. This could be just the thing I need. The way these two are looking at each other, I might not have to do much but sit back and watch. Love will give the man something to be grateful for.

But as the evening winds down and Evan prepares to take his leave, I sense a shift in the energy, a heaviness settling over his spirit. *Rats.* So much for doing nothing.

I follow him to the front door, slipping outside and positioning myself beneath the snow-laden eaves to listen as he and Molly say their goodbyes.

"Thank you again for dinner, Molly," Evan says, his voice warm and sincere. "It was wonderful, truly. I haven't felt this welcomed and at ease in a long time."

Good, good, this is good.

Molly smiles sweetly, her hand brushing against Evan's arm in a friendly gesture. "You're always welcome here, Evan. Chad and I, we really enjoy your company."

Evan swallows, a flicker of something vulnerable and unguarded in his eyes. "I enjoy your company too, Molly. More than I've enjoyed anything in a long time. But..."

"But what?" Molly prompts gently, her head tilting in concern.

Evan sighs, his breath forming a cloud of frost in the chill night air. "But..." He pauses. "Nothing." His shoulders drop as he tucks his hands in his pockets. Invisible walls seem to go up all around him. "Thanks again for dinner."

Molly is quiet for a moment, her gaze drifting out over the snow-covered lawn, but doesn't seem to take offense. When she speaks, her voice is filled with a gentle understanding. "You're welcome." She smiles. "Like I said, you're welcome anytime."

With a final, grateful nod, Evan turns and makes his way down the path, his footsteps crunching in the freshly fallen snow. I watch him go, my heart swelling with a mix of hope and understanding. Evan isn't sure how to let someone in or perhaps, he's been so consumed with what he believes his unfair lot in life is, he can't see he's surrounded by blessings.

But that's where I come in... and with a little help from Molly and Chad, we just might pull off this Christmas miracle.

As his truck rumbles to life and pulls away from the curb, I close my eyes, reaching out with my angelic senses to offer a small blessing, a gentle nudge towards the light. In the distance, I feel the stirring of a thankful heart; a neighbor moved to express their gratitude for the beauty Evan brings to their lives through his Christmas tree farm.

It's a tiny ripple, a whisper of hope in the vast tapestry of Evan's journey. But it's a start, a reminder that even in his moments of doubt and hesitation, he is appreciated; he is valued; he is making a difference.

With a soft sigh, I step back from the window, feeling the familiar tug of the celestial realm calling me home. In a shimmering blink, I find myself back in the Loom of Light, my place of employment in the heavenly realm, where the gentle hum of creation washes over me like a soothing balm.

But as I settle at my workstation, my fingers poised to

weave the delicate strands of a new robe, I feel a flicker of frustration, a nagging sense of inadequacy. The threads seem to tangle and knot beneath my touch, my stitches uneven and clumsy.

"Why is this so hard?" I mutter to myself, my brow furrowed in concentration. In my earthly life, I could barely thread a needle, but I've been stitching these things for more than a year now. "I thought I was getting the hang of it, but it feels like I'm right back at square one."

"Patience, my dear Betty," a warm voice chuckles behind me. I turn to see Henry, his wise eyes twinkling with understanding. "You're being too hard on yourself. This is a journey, remember? For both you and Evan. There will be stumbles and setbacks, but that's all part of the process."

I bite my lip, feeling the sting of tears prickling at the corners of my eyes. He's not talking about my sewing capabilities. "I know, Henry. But it's just...it's harder than I thought.

Henry lays a comforting hand on my shoulder, his touch radiating a soothing warmth. "I know Betty. But you are learning, growing, just as Evan is. And the fact that you care so deeply, that you want so badly to make a difference, that is your greatest strength, your most powerful gift."

I take a shuddering breath, letting Henry's words wash over me like a cleansing rain. "You're right, Henry. I know you are. It's just hard to remember sometimes, amid all the doubts and frustrations."

"I know, my dear. Believe me, I know. But that's why we have each other, why we have this sacred space to return to when the earthly realm feels overwhelming. Here, we can recharge, refocus, and remember the truth of who we are and what we're called to do."

I nod, feeling a flicker of hope reigniting in my chest. "Thank you, Henry. I don't know what I'd do without your guidance, your wisdom."

Henry chuckles, patting my hand gently. "Oh, I have no doubt you'd find your way, Betty. You have a strength and resilience that is truly remarkable. But I'm honored to walk beside you on this journey, to offer what support I can."

With a final squeeze of my shoulder, Henry moves off to check on the other apprentices, leaving me alone with my thoughts and my loom. I take a deep breath, centering myself in the present moment, in the sacred task before me.

"Alright, Evan," I whisper, my fingers moving with renewed purpose over the luminous threads. "I know you're unsure, I know you're hesitant. But I also know that you have so much love to give, so much joy waiting to be discovered. And I promise, I will be here every step of the way, guiding you, supporting you, believing in you. Even when you can't believe in yourself."

As I work, I feel a sense of peace settling over me, a deep trust in the unfolding of Evan's journey. I may not have all the answers, may not be able to fix everything with a snap of my fingers. But I have faith, I have hope, and I have the unwavering conviction that every soul is worthy of love, of healing, of the chance to become their truest, most radiant self.

And that is the true miracle of Christmas, the true gift of this sacred season. The reminder that we are never alone, never without guidance and support. That there is always a hand reaching out to us, always a voice whispering words of comfort and encouragement.

I step back from my loom, ready to return to the earthly realm and continue my mission of love and service. I feel a deep sense of gratitude, a profound awe at the mystery and magic of it all.

For in this moment, I understand the true meaning of my calling, the true purpose of my angelic journey. It's not about perfection, not about forcing or controlling or having all the answers.

It's about love. Pure, patient, compassionate love. The kind of love that meets each soul exactly where they are, that honors the unique path and timing of every individual journey.

Five

EVAN

The sun hasn't even peeked over the horizon when my phone buzzes, jolting me out of a restless sleep. I groan, fumbling for the device on my nightstand, my eyes squinting against the harsh glow of the screen.

It's a text from Molly: **Evan, I'm so sorry to bother you this early, but my car won't start. I'm going to be late for my shift at the diner, and I have no idea how I'm going to get Chad to school. Is there any chance you could help?**

I sit up, rubbing the sleep from my eyes, a pang of concern tugging at my chest. Molly is on her own, working herself to the bone to provide for her son. The last thing she needs is car trouble on top of everything else.

I text back quickly, my fingers clumsy with sleep: **No problem at all. I'll be there in 15 minutes to give you a ride. Don't worry about a thing.**

I throw on some clothes, not even bothering to check

if they match, and head out to my truck. The air is frigid; the windshield frosted over, and I curse under my breath as I wait for the defroster to kick in.

As I drive through the quiet streets of Benton Falls, the Christmas lights twinkling in the early morning darkness, I can't help but feel a twinge of envy. All these people, safe and warm in their homes, living their perfect little lives. They have no idea what it's like to feel trapped, to dream of a life beyond the confines of this small town.

But then I think of Molly, of the strength and resilience she shows every single day, and I feel a flush of shame. Who am I to complain about my lot in life when she's working so hard just to keep her head above water?

I pull up to her house, the porch light casting a warm glow in the predawn gloom. Molly comes out, Chad trailing behind her, both of them bundled up against the cold.

"Evan," Molly says, her voice filled with relief and gratitude. "Thank you so much for coming. I don't know what I would have done without you."

I wave off her thanks, feeling a warmth spread through my chest that has nothing to do with the heater blasting in the truck. "It's no trouble at all, Molly. I'm just glad I could help."

Chad scrambles into the back seat, his eyes wide with excitement. "Wow, Mr. Evan. Your truck is so cool! Can I honk the horn?"

I chuckle, glancing at Molly as she climbs into the passenger seat. "Maybe later, buddy. For now, let's focus on getting you to school on time."

As I drive, Molly fills me in on her car troubles, her brow furrowed with worry. "I just don't know how I'm going to afford the repairs," she says, her voice tight. "With Christmas coming up, and Chad's winter coat getting too small, and the rent due next week..."

She trails off, her eyes glistening with unshed tears. I reach over, giving her hand a gentle squeeze. "Hey, it's going to be okay. We'll figure something out. I know a guy at the auto shop who owes me a favor. I'm sure he can give you a good deal on the repairs."

Molly looks at me, her eyes filled with a mix of hope and uncertainty. "Evan, I can't ask you to do that. You've already done so much for us."

I shake my head, a smile tugging at the corner of my mouth. "You're not asking, I'm offering. That's what friends are for, right?"

The word "friends" feels strange on my tongue, foreign and unfamiliar. I've been so focused on my own problems, my own dreams of escape, that I've forgotten what it's like to have people in my life who I care about, who I want to help.

Chad pipes up from the back seat, his voice filled with childlike wonder. "Mr. Evan, are you and my mom best friends now? Because that would be awesome!"

I glance at Molly, seeing the hint of a blush coloring her cheeks. "Yeah, buddy," I say, my voice low. "I guess we are."

We drop Chad off at school, watching as he bounds up the steps, his backpack bouncing with each step. Molly watches him go, a tender smile on her face, and I feel a sudden, fierce urge to protect her, to shield her from all the hardships and heartaches that life has thrown her way.

But as we drive to the diner, the silence stretching between us; I feel the old frustrations creeping back in. The restlessness, the yearning for something more than this small-town life.

"I envy you, you know," I blurt out, the words tumbling from my mouth before I can stop them. "Not that your car won't start, but that you have this whole world of possibilities open to you, this chance to start fresh and chase your dreams. You aren't bound by the expectations of others. Here I am, stuck on a Christmas tree farm in the middle of nowhere, watching life pass me by because I wasn't given a say in the matter."

Molly is quiet for a moment, her gaze fixed on the passing storefronts. When she speaks, her voice is gentle but filled with a quiet strength. "Evan, I know it might not seem like it, but you have possibilities too. You have a chance to make this farm into something truly special, to build a life here that's filled with purpose and meaning."

I snort, the sound harsh in the stillness of the truck. "Easy for you to say. You're not the one saddled with a family legacy you never asked for, a life you never chose."

Molly reaches over, her hand resting on my arm. The touch is gentle, almost hesitant, but it sends a jolt of electricity through me. "I understand feeling trapped, feeling like your life isn't your own. Believe me, I do. But I've also learned that sometimes, the greatest adventures, the deepest joys, are waiting for us right where we are.

We just have to open our eyes and our hearts to see them."

Her words hang in the air between us, a challenge and an invitation all at once. I want to believe her, want to trust in the possibility of happiness, of contentment. But the old doubts, the old fears, cling to me like cobwebs, clouding my vision and my judgment.

We pull up to the diner, the warm glow of the windows a beacon in the early morning darkness. Molly turns to me, her eyes searching my face. "Thank you again, Evan. For everything. I don't know what I would've done without you today."

I nod, my throat tight with emotion. "Anytime, Molly. I mean it."

She gives me one last smile, then slips out of the truck, hurrying towards the diner's entrance. I watch her go, feeling a tug in my chest, a longing for something I can't quite name.

As I drive back to the farm, the sun just peeking over the horizon, I try to shake off the melancholy, the sense of dissatisfaction that clings to me like a second skin. I have work to do, trees to tend, a business to run. I can't afford to get lost in daydreams and what-ifs.

But as I pull into the driveway, the familiar sight of the barn and the rows of evergreens stretching out before me, I feel a flicker of something I haven't felt in a long time.

Hope.

It's small, fragile, like a candle flame in a windstorm.

But it's there, a tiny spark of possibility in the darkness of my doubts.

I think of Molly's words, of her unwavering belief in the power of the present moment, the potential for joy and meaning right here, right now. And I feel a sudden, fierce desire to prove her right. To find a way to make this farm, this life, into something I can be proud of. Something I can love.

I climb out of the truck, the brisk morning air filling my lungs, the scent of pine and wood smoke tickling my nose. The farm is quiet, peaceful, the only sound the gentle rustling of the wind through the trees.

I take a deep breath, squaring my shoulders, a new sense of determination settling over me. I may not have all the answers, may not know exactly where this journey will lead me. But for the first time in longer than I can remember, I'm ready to find out.

Ready to take a chance on the life I have, instead of pining for the one I don't.

I head towards the barn, my mind already racing with ideas, with plans. I'll start with the little things, the small improvements that can make a big difference. A fresh coat of paint on the barn, some new signs to guide customers through the trees. Maybe even a hot cocoa stand, a place for families to gather and warm up after a long day of searching for the perfect tree.

As I gather my tools, the first rays of sunlight filtering through the dusty windows, I feel a smile spreading across my face. It's a strange feeling, this flicker of excitement, of anticipation. But it's a welcome one, a reminder that even in the darkest of times, there's always a glimmer of hope waiting to be found.

The day passes in a blur of activity, my mind and body fully engaged in the work at hand. I trim branches, stack firewood, even start sketching out designs for a new wreath-making station. It's hard work, physical and mental, but it feels good. Honest. Like I'm finally putting my energy into something that matters.

As the sun dips below the tree line, casting long shadows across the farm, I hear the crunch of tires on gravel. I look up to see Molly's battered old sedan pulling into the driveway, Chad waving excitedly from the passenger seat.

I feel a flutter of nervousness in my stomach, a sudden self-consciousness about my dirt-streaked face and sweat-stained shirt. But then Molly steps out of the car, a warm smile on her face, and all my worries melt away.

"Evan, hi!" she says, her voice bright with surprise. "I hope we're not interrupting anything."

I shake my head, wiping my hands on my jeans. "Not at all. I was just finishing up for the day. What brings you out here?"

Chad bounds over, his eyes wide with excitement. "Mr. Evan, Mom said we could come visit you at the farm. Can you show me how to cut down a tree? Can I help you make a wreath? Can we have a campfire and roast marshmallows?"

I laugh, ruffling his hair affectionately. "Whoa there, buddy. Let's take it one step at a time. I don't want you handling any sharp tools just yet. But I'd be happy to let you help me stack some wood, maybe make a wreath. How does that sound?"

Chad nods eagerly, practically vibrating with enthusiasm. "Yes, please. I want to learn everything about being a Christmas tree farmer."

Molly watches us, a tender expression on her face. "I hope you don't mind us dropping in like this. I just wanted to say thank you for the ride this morning and thanks for putting in a good word with your friend." She smiles and I can't breathe while she's looking at me like that. "He had my car ready by the time my shift was over."

I meet her gaze. My pulse picks up as I search her eyes. "I'm glad to hear it."

She smiles, her eyes crinkling at the corners, and I feel a sudden, overwhelming urge to reach out and touch her. To pull her close and breathe in the scent of her hair, the softness of her skin.

But I resist pushing the thought away. We're friends, nothing more. And I'm not looking for one more reason to be tied to this town, even if that reason has the most captivating hazel eyes I've ever seen.

Instead, I turn to Chad, clapping him on the shoulder. "All right, buddy. Let's get to work, shall we? Maybe your mom can work on a wreath for you to take home while we finish stacking the wood."

Chad giggles, his face lighting up with mischief. "Okay."

I'm surprised by Chad's enthusiasm to stack wood,

but then I'm reminded of when I was a young boy, happy to do anything with my dad on the farm.

As we set off towards the barn, Molly falls into step beside me, and I feel a sense of rightness settle over me. I'm glad there aren't any customers to take me away from this moment.

Just inside the doorway of the barn, I show Molly the pile of boughs, cut wire, and tools needed to create a wreath of her own. "Go ahead and get started. It won't take us long to stack this wood."

As the sun sets behind the mountains, painting the sky in shades of pink and gold, we finish up the woodpile and make our way inside the barn. Chad is dragging his feet now, his energy flagging after a long day of excitement and adventure. Molly is holding up a beautiful wreath, admiring her work.

"Wow," I look at the perfectly symmetrical circle of evergreen branches. "You didn't tell me you were an expert wreath builder."

Molly's cheeks blush and I search for anything else to say to keep the flush of happiness on her face. "I'm not, but this was so much fun."

"You want a job?" I asked, half serious, but suddenly the idea is the best one I've had in years. Molly raises a brow, her eyes searching mine. She can't tell if I'm joking or not. "Seriously." A plan formulates in my mind. "You can work here as little or as much as you'd like when you're not at the diner. The pay isn't monumental, but I'll do the best I can. And I'd be happy to keep Chad here with me after school."

I can see the thought racing through her mind. "Just for the holiday season. I think it would help both of us out."

She brushes the hair back from her face. "I...I... I think that would be amazing." Her eyes are glowing, and I can't tell if they're lit with emotion or barn light. "You're an answer to a prayer."

Chad tugs on his mom's sleeve. "Do we get to work for Mr. Evan?" His tired eyes brighten. Molly scoops him up, balancing him on her hip with a practiced ease. "I think so." She glances at me, and I exhale. "But first we better get you home to bed," she says, her voice warm with affection.

I nod, feeling a pang of disappointment at the thought of saying goodbye. "I'll see you tomorrow?"

She smiles, her eyes searching mine. "I've got the morning shift, but we can come after I pick Chad up from school."

"That'll be great." I can already feel the anticipation for tomorrow, like a seedling ready to sprout.

We stand there for a moment; the silence stretching between us, heavy with unspoken words and unspoken feelings. Then Chad yawns, his head drooping against Molly's shoulder, and the spell is broken.

"I should get him home," Molly says, her voice soft with regret. "See you tomorrow."

I nod, a smile tugging at the corner of my mouth. "See you then."

As I watch them drive away, the taillights of Molly's car disappearing into the gathering dusk, I head back to the barn, my mind already racing with plans for tomorrow.

Suddenly, the tree farm feels new and exciting, and it's all because of Molly and Chad. Perhaps there's hope for even a grumpy old Scrooge like me finding his Christmas spirit.

I smile to myself, shaking my head at the thought. It's a cheesy sentiment, the kind you'd find on a holiday card or a made-for-TV movie. But somehow, standing here in the fading light of a December evening, it feels true.

Feels right.

I take one last look around the farm, at the trees and the barn and the house that's waiting for me just beyond and for the first time in a very long time, I'm happy to be home.

Six

BETTY

The chilly December air fills my lungs as I appear at the edge of Evan's Christmas tree farm, the scent of foliage and damp earth mingling in a fragrant dance. It's early, the sun just beginning its steady rise, but already I can sense the stirring of life, the gentle hum of anticipation that heralds the start of another day.

I walk among the rows of trees, my fingers trailing over the frost-kissed needles, marveling at the way they glisten in the nascent light. Each one is a tiny miracle, a witness to the power of nature, of growth, of the indomitable spirit that drives all living things to reach for the heavens.

And yet, as I attune my angelic senses to the farm's energy, I feel an undercurrent of restlessness, of discontent. It's Evan, I know, his spirit still yearning for something more, something beyond the confines of this small-town life.

I sigh, my heart aching for this lost soul who can't see

the beauty, the purpose, the sheer magic that surrounds him. If only I could open his eyes, help him understand that true happiness, true fulfillment, lies not in some distant horizon, but in the here and now, in the love and connection and sense of belonging that's waiting for him, if only he'd let it in.

But I know it's not that simple. Evan's journey is his own, his choices, his revelations, not mine to control or dictate. All I can do is guide, support, and pray that somehow, someway, he'll find his way to the life, the love he's meant for.

As if in answer to my silent plea, I feel a sudden shift in the air, a ripple of joy and excitement that makes my angelic heart soar. I turn, my eyes widening as I see Molly's car pulling up the gravel drive, Chad bouncing in his seat, his face pressed against the window in eager anticipation.

They're here, and I can't help but think about the woman and child who hold the key to Evan's healing, to his happiness. The ones who can show him, better than I ever could, the true meaning of Christmas, of family, of home.

I close my eyes, reaching out with my celestial senses, weaving a gentle blessing into the early morning air. Let them see the beauty in this place, the potential, the promise. Let their love, their laughter, their unshakeable belief in the goodness of life be the beacon that guides Evan back to the light.

When I open my eyes, Molly and Chad are already out of the car, their cheeks flushed with cold and excitement. Molly is wearing a cozy red sweater and a pair of well-worn jeans, her chestnut hair escaping from beneath a knit hat in wispy tendrils. Chad is a bundle of energy, his puffy blue coat making him look like a miniature marshmallow as he darts among the trees, his laughter ringing out like silver bells.

"Mom, look!" he calls, pointing to a towering Douglas fir. "It's taller than our house!"

Molly laughs, the sound warm and rich and full of love. "It sure is, buddy. It's as all as the one in the town square."

As they continue to explore, exclaiming over each new discovery, I catch a glimpse of Evan emerging from the barn, his dark hair tousled, his blue eyes still heavy with sleep. But as he spots Molly and Chad, a smile blooms across his face, bright and genuine, chasing away the shadows that always seem to linger in his gaze.

"Well, well, well," he calls, striding towards them, his boots crunching in the snow. "If it isn't my two favorite new employees."

Molly grins, her eyes sparkling with mischief. "We're ready to get to work."

Evan's eyebrows shoot up as a wide smile cuts across his face. "I'm glad to hear it, but I thought you weren't coming until the afternoon. Didn't you have a morning shift at the diner? And doesn't Chad have school?"

Molly smiles sheepishly, "I forgot it was teacher prep day, so no school for the students. Luckily, I checked the calendar before bed last night. I switched my shift to the evening shift and was hoping you wouldn't mind your employees showing up early."

Evan smiles and points at the barn. "Of course I don't mind, I've got your wreath making station all set up."

As they head towards the barn, chattering and laughing, I feel a swell of warmth in my chest, a glimmer of hope that maybe, just maybe, this will be the day that everything changes. The day that Evan sees the farm, not as a burden, but as a blessing, a chance to create something beautiful, something lasting, with the people he loves.

I decide now is the perfect opportunity to spend some quality time with my assignment. "Hello there." I call out as I approach them.

Evan turns, his eyes lighting with recognition. "Oh, hello—Barb..."

"Betty," I interject. "How are you Evan?"

"Good." He smiles and I'm glad he remembers me. "Betty, this is Molly and her son Chad."

"It's nice to meet you Betty." Molly smiles, the gesture illuminating her eyes. I can feel her sweet spirit emanating all around her. No wonder Evan likes her so much.

"You too," I add as I wave at Chad, who offers me a big toothy grin, making me miss my grandson. I silently promise to check in on him later; send him a little angel love.

"Are you in need of a tree?" Evan asks.

"Oh, no." I reach inside my pocket and feel the

Miracle Card. Now's not the right time to use it, but it's reassuring to know it's there. "I came to see if you could use a volunteer." I exhale as 3 vehicles, full of eager Christmas Tree enthusiasts, pull into the parking area.

Evan glances at the trucks, then at me. "Yes," he scratches at the wool cap on his head. "It looks like I could some extra help." He smiles at me. "Talk about perfect timing."

"It's kind of my thing." I grin. "Where would you like me?"

Evan looks over as his latest customers emerge from the vehicles and wander towards the rows of trees. "I'll go help them, if you'll go into the barn and help Molly get started on some wreaths." His eyes meet Molly's—the connection between them is palpable—"I've got a feeling we're going to need as many wreaths as we can get."

"Sounds great." I'm excited to do something other than sew.

"I'll be back as soon as I can." Evan nods and takes off towards the customers.

I follow Molly inside, the scent of pine and cinnamon enveloping me like a hug. There are a couple of other employees bustling about, hanging garlands, stacking firewood, and arranging displays of ornaments and trinkets. In the center of it all is a large wooden table, piled high with evergreen boughs, ribbons, and wire.

"You must be the new employees." A giant of a man with a handlebar mustache makes his way over. "Evan said you'd be coming today."

Molly looks up, followed by Chad's exaggerated stare.

"I'm Molly, and this is my son Chad."

"And I'm Betty, volunteering for the day," I add.

"Glad to have you. I'm Paul and that over there is Seth." He glances towards the man standing on the ladder hanging garland. Seth nods in our direction.

"Evan asked us to make wreaths." Molly looks at the table, then at me. "We better get started."

I agree as Paul invites Chad to help stack the extra cut boughs for wreaths. Chad looks at his mom for permission, then marches off behind Paul, a little spring to his step.

Molly and I go to the table. "I've never made a wreath before." I admit. Suddenly my robe-making insecurities surface. Maybe I'd better help Chad.

"That's okay. It's really simple." Molly slips her coat off and hangs it on a nearby chair. "Wreath-making 101. The first thing you need to know is that it's all about the base. You want to start with a good, sturdy frame, something that will hold up to all the decorations you're going to pile on top."

She reaches for a coil of wire, her fingers deft and sure as she shapes it into a circle. "See, like this. Nice and tight, but not too tight. You want it to have a little give, a little flexibility."

I watch her work, not truly convinced this is something I can do. "You make it look so easy," I murmur as I reach out to touch a sprig of holly.

Molly grins, handing me the wire frame. "That's because it is easy once you get the hang of it. Here, you try."

As I weave the greenery around the wire, my brow furrowed in concentration, Evan steps into the barn. "How's it going?"

"Just got started." Molly gets to work. I sense Evan's gaze lingering on her face, tracing the curve of her cheek, the fullness of her lips. There's a tenderness in his eyes, a longing that makes my angelic heart flutter with anticipation.

Oh, my dear boy, if you only knew how much she cares for you, how much light and love she could bring into your life, if only you'd let her.

But Evan looks away, his expression clouding over, and I can feel the old doubts, the old fears, creeping back in. He's still holding himself back, still clinging to the idea that he doesn't deserve happiness, that he's somehow betraying his family, his legacy, by even daring to dream of a different life.

I want to reach out, to shake him, to shout in his ear that he's wrong, that he's worthy, that he's loved. But I know it's not my place, not my role. All I can do is watch, and pray, and hope that somehow, someway, he'll find the courage to open his heart, to take the leap of faith that will change everything.

"I better get back out there. If you need anything, just ask Paul or Seth." Evan straightens his shoulders. "It's going to be a busy day."

As the morning wears on, more customers arrive, families and couples and groups of friends, all eager to find the perfect tree, the perfect wreath, the perfect little piece of Christmas magic to take home with them. Evan moves among them, greeting each one with a smile and a kind word, his eyes crinkling at the corners as he listens to their stories, their laughter, their dreams.

And as he does, I can feel something shifting in him, a softening, a warming, like the first tentative blooms of spring after a long, hard winter. He's starting to see the farm through their eyes, through Molly's eyes, to understand the joy, the wonder, the sheer delight that it brings to so many hearts.

It's a small change, a subtle one, but it's there, growing stronger with every passing moment. And as I watch him, as I feel the love, the gratitude, the pure, unbridled happiness radiating from every soul he touches, I can't stop myself from smiling, my own spirit lifting knowing that maybe, just maybe, my work here is not in vain.

But even as I revel in the progress, in the glimmers of hope and healing, I can't shake the feeling that something is still holding Evan back, some deep-seated pain or fear that he's not yet ready to face. And so, I close my eyes once more, reaching out with all the love, all the compassion, all the divine guidance that my angelic heart can muster.

Show him, I whisper to heaven above, to the great force that moves us all. Show him the truth of who he is, of what he's meant to be. Give him the strength, the courage, the faith to let go of the past and embrace the beautiful, boundless future that awaits him.

For a moment, there is only silence, a stillness so profound that it feels like the entire world is holding its breath. And then, as if in answer to my prayer, I hear Molly's voice, kind and gentle, drifting across the barn like a summer breeze.

"Evan," she says, her hand coming to rest on his arm. "Can I ask you something?"

He turns to her, his brow furrowed, his eyes searching her face. "Of course. Anything."

She hesitates, biting her lip, as if gathering her courage. "I was just wondering... what made you decide to take over the farm? I mean, I know it's been in your family for generations, but... was it always your dream, to be here, to do this work?"

Evan stiffens, his jaw clenching, and for a moment, I'm afraid he's going to shut down, to push her away. But then, something in him seems to crumble, his shoulders sagging, his eyes filling with a weariness, a vulnerability, that I've never seen before.

"No," he says, his voice hoarse, barely above a whisper. "No, it wasn't my dream. It was my father's, and his father's, before him. But dad's body was wearing out and he couldn't manage the farm anymore, and I didn't see any other choice. My brother's in the military, he can't be here, and my mom... she needs to be with my dad. They deserve to enjoy these years together. So I stepped up, I took on the responsibility. Because that's what you do, right? That's what family means."

Molly nods, her eyes shining with understanding, with empathy. "Of course. Of course it is. But Evan... that doesn't mean you have to give up on your own dreams, your own happiness."

Evan looks at her, his expression raw, stripped bare, and I can see the war raging within him, the desperate, aching longing to believe her, to trust in the possibility of something more. "It's hard to chase after your own dreams when you're living someone else's."

Molly smiles, her hand tightening on his arm, her eyes holding his with a fierce, unwavering compassion. "I think sometimes we get caught up in what we think we're missing out on, I've seen you handle the trees with such tenderness and care, and I've seen the way you talk with your customers, if I didn't know better I'd say this is your dream." She studies his face. "Evan, what you're doing here matters. *You* matter to this town," Molly pauses. "To me."

And with those words, something in Evan seems to break open. "Thank you," he murmurs, his voice thick with emotion. "I really needed to hear that."

And as they stand there, lost in each other, in the perfect, shining moment of connection and understanding, I feel a warmth blooming in my chest, a light so bright, so pure, that it feels like the very essence of heaven itself.

It turns out there are angels on earth and Molly is one of them.

And as I watch them, as I feel the love, the joy, the sheer, incandescent hope radiating from every fiber of their beings, I know that my work here is not finished, but it has reached a turning point.

A new chapter, a new beginning, full of promise and possibility.

Seven

EVAN

The morning sun peeks through the frosty windows of my cabin, casting a warm glow across the rough-hewn floorboards. I stretch, my muscles still aching from yesterday's work at the farm, but there's a lightness in my chest that I can't quite explain.

As I go through my morning routine, my mind keeps drifting back to yesterday, to the laughter and warmth and easy camaraderie of spending the day with Molly and Chad. I can't remember the last time I felt so content, so at peace with the world around me.

It's a strange feeling, this flicker of hope, this whisper of possibility. For so long, I've been focused on what I don't have, on the dreams that always seemed just out of reach. But now, as I think about Molly and Chad, about the joy they bring to my life, I wonder if maybe, just maybe, my dreams have been right in front of me all along.

I shake my head, a rueful smile tugging at my lips.

Listen to me, getting all sentimental and introspective. If my buddies from high school could see me now, they'd never let me hear the end of it.

But as I step outside, the cold December air filling my lungs, I can't deny the truth of what I'm feeling. The farm, this town, this life—it's not what I planned, not what I thought I wanted. But maybe, if things continue with Molly and Chad, it could be something more. Something better.

Later that evening, I'm still lost in thought as I make my way into town, the streets already buzzing with excitement for the annual tree lighting ceremony. It's a Benton Falls tradition, one that brings the whole community together to celebrate the start of the holiday season.

As I walk, I wave at Betty, who is across the square just before I catch sight of Molly and Chad up ahead, huddled together against the cold. Chad is bouncing on his toes, his eyes wide with anticipation, while Molly looks on with a fond, indulgent smile.

"Evan!" Chad calls out, waving me over with a grin. "You made it!"

I chuckle, ruffling his hair as I join them. "Wouldn't miss it for the world, buddy. I hear Santa himself is going to be making an appearance."

Chad's eyes go wide, his mouth falling open in a perfect little 'o' of wonder. "Really? Do you think he'll remember what I asked for? I wrote him a letter and everything!"

Molly laughs, wrapping an arm around his shoulders

and pulling him close. "I'm sure he will, sweetie. Santa never forgets a request from a true believer."

I watch them together, feeling a warmth bloom in my chest. There's just something about seeing Molly in full-on mom mode that gets to me, that makes me feel like I'm a part of something special, something real.

As if sensing my gaze, Molly glances up, her hazel eyes meeting mine. For a moment, it's like the rest of the world falls away, like there's nothing but the two of us, lost in the spell of the twinkling lights and the melodious strains of holiday music.

But then someone calls my name, breaking the moment, and I turn to see a familiar face pushing through the crowd.

"Evan Lawson, is that you?"

I blink, my brain taking a second to catch up. "Morgan? Morgan Caldwell?"

She grins, throwing her arms around me in a quick hug. "The one and only. Wow, it's been ages. How have you been?"

I return the hug, a little dazed. Morgan and I went to high school together, but I haven't seen her since graduation. Last I heard, she'd left Benton Falls to chase her dreams of being a big-shot TV producer in the city.

"I've been good," I say, stepping back to get a better look at her. She looks different, more polished and put-together than the girl I remember. "Just been keeping busy with the farm, you know how it is."

Morgan nods, her gaze flicking to Molly and Chad. "I

heard you took over your family's place. That's great, Evan. Really great."

But there's something in her voice, a hint of pity or condescension, that sets my teeth on edge. Like she can't quite believe that I'm still here, still tied to this small-town life, while she's out there living the dream.

"And who's this?" she asks, turning her attention to Molly and Chad with a bright, curious smile.

I clear my throat, suddenly feeling awkward and unsure. "Oh, um, this is Molly and her son, Chad. They're... we're..."

I trail off, not quite knowing how to define what we are. Friends? Something more? The words stick in my throat, heavy and clumsy.

But Molly, bless her, steps in to save me. "We're good friends," she says warmly, extending a hand to Morgan. "Evan's been kind enough to let Chad and I help at the farm this year. It's been a real lifesaver, honestly."

Morgan takes her hand, shaking it with a smile that doesn't quite reach her eyes. "How nice," she says, her voice sugary sweet. "I'm sure Evan's just thrilled to have the extra help. Running that farm all by himself must be quite the challenge."

I bristle at her tone, at the implication that I'm somehow struggling, that I need to be pitied or saved. But before I can say anything, Chad pipes up, his voice bright with excitement.

"Evan's the best." He declares, bouncing on his toes. "He knows everything about Christmas trees, and he even let me help make a wreath yesterday. It was so cool."

Morgan's smile softens, becoming a little more genuine. "That does sound cool, buddy. You're a lucky kid, getting to spend so much time with Evan. He's one of the good ones."

I feel a flush creep up my neck, equal parts pleased and embarrassed by the praise. Morgan and I were never close, but we ran in the same circles, and I always got the sense that she thought I was a bit of a screw-up, a small-town boy with small-town dreams.

To hear her say something nice about me now, after all these years, feels strange. Like she's reassessing, seeing me in a new light.

"Thanks, Morgan," I say gruffly, shoving my hands in my pockets. "I'm the lucky one, really. Molly and Chad, they're... they're pretty special."

I glance at Molly as I say it, feeling a rush of warmth at the sweet, surprised smile that touches her lips. She holds my gaze for a moment, her eyes shining with something I can't quite name, before turning back to Morgan.

"So, what brings you back to Benton Falls?" she asks, her voice light and friendly. "Just here for the holidays, or...?"

Morgan laughs, a little too loudly. "Oh, no. I could never stay away from the city for that long. I'm a television producer and my news team was assigned to cover the gingerbread house contest. We're out of here as soon as we wrap."

She says it casually, like it's no big deal, but I can hear the unspoken message beneath her words. That she's outgrown this place, this life. That she's moved on to bigger and better things, while the rest of us are still stuck in the same old rut.

It stings more than it should, this reminder of everything I've ever wanted for myself. The travel, the adventure, the chance to make something of myself beyond the boundaries of Benton Falls.

For a moment, I feel a hot flare of envy in my gut, a sudden, desperate longing for the freedom that Morgan has, the choices and opportunities that she gets to take for granted.

But then I feel a small hand slip into mine, and I look down to see Chad grinning up at me, his eyes bright with trust and affection. And just like that, the envy fades, replaced by a rush of gratitude, of warmth, of something that might just be love.

I squeeze Chad's hand, feeling a smile tug at my lips. "Hey, buddy, what do you say we go check out the hot cocoa stand? I hear they've got peppermint flavor this year."

He whoops with excitement, tugging me towards the stand with an exuberant "Come on, Evan."

Molly and I exchange a look of fond amusement as we let ourselves be pulled along in his wake. I wave goodbye to Morgan.

"He's a good kid," I murmur to Molly as we wait in line, the sweet scent of chocolate and mint wafting through the air.

Molly smiles, her shoulder brushing mine as she leans into me. "He is," she agrees. "And he thinks the world of you, Evan."

EVAN

I swallow hard, suddenly feeling unsteady on my feet. It's one thing to know, in my heart, how I feel about Molly and Chad. But to hear her say it, to know that they feel the same way...

It's terrifying and exhilarating all at once, like standing on the edge of a cliff, ready to take the leap into something new, something unknown.

But before I can respond, it's our turn to order, and the moment passes, lost in the chaos of choosing toppings and juggling steaming cups of cocoa.

As we sip our drinks and watch the ceremony unfold, I can't shake the feeling of unease that Morgan's words have stirred up in me. The nagging sense that maybe she's right, that maybe I am settling, giving up on my dreams for the security of the familiar.

I glance at Molly, taking in the soft curve of her cheek, the way the twinkling lights dance in her eyes. She looks happy, content in a way that I envy. Like she's exactly where she's meant to be.

"How do you do it?" I ask suddenly, the words tumbling out before I can stop them. "How do you stay so positive, so hopeful, even when life doesn't turn out the way you planned?"

Molly looks at me, surprise flickering across her face. "What do you mean?"

I hesitate, not sure how to put my tangled thoughts into words. "I just... I know you've been through a lot, Molly. With your ex, and being a single mom, and working so hard to make ends meet. But you never seem to let it get you down. You're always smiling, always looking on the bright side. How do you do it?"

Molly is quiet for a moment, her gaze turning inward. "It's not always easy," she admits. "There are days when I want to give up, when I wonder if I'm doing the right thing, if I'm strong enough to keep going on my own."

She takes a sip of her cocoa, her breath fogging in the cold air. "But then I look at Chad, at the life we've built together, and I remember how lucky I am. I have a beautiful son, a job I love, friends who care about me. And maybe it's not the life I always imagined for myself, but it's a good life. A life worth being grateful for."

I nod slowly, turning her words over in my mind. "But don't you ever wonder about the road not taken? About what else might be out there, waiting for you?"

Molly smiles, a little sadly. "Of course I do. Everyone does. But dwelling on what might have been... it's a waste of energy. All we can do is make the best of what we have, and trust that we're exactly where we're meant to be."

I fall silent, mulling over her words. There's a wisdom, a strength in them I can't help but admire. But there's a part of me that rebels against the idea of just accepting my lot in life. That yearns for something more, something different.

"I guess I just... I don't want to wake up one day and realize I've let my whole life pass me by," I say quietly. "I don't want to have regrets, to wonder what I might have achieved if I'd just had the courage to chase my dreams."

Molly looks at me, her eyes searching mine. "And

what are your dreams, Evan? What is it you want, more than anything?"

I open my mouth to answer, but the words won't come. Because the truth is, I'm not sure anymore. For so long, my dreams have been a vague, distant thing. The idea of escape, of adventure, of a life beyond the confines of Benton Falls.

But standing here, with Molly and Chad by my side, I'm wondering if maybe my dreams have been closer than I've realized. If maybe the things I've been running from are the very things that could make me happy, if I just let them.

"I don't know," I admit hoarsely. "I thought I did, but now... now I'm not so sure."

Molly nods, understanding flickering in her eyes. "That's okay," she says. "You don't have to have all the answers, Evan. No one does. But don't be so afraid of making the wrong choice that you miss out on the happiness that's right in front of you."

I swallow hard, feeling a sudden, irrational surge of anger. "That's easy for you to say," I snap. "You're the one who's always so content, so at peace with your life. But some of us want more, Molly. Some of us need more."

Molly recoils as if I've slapped her, hurt flashing across her face. "You think I don't want more?" she asks, her voice trembling. "You think I don't have dreams, hopes, things I wish I could change about my life?"

She shakes her head, tears welling in her eyes. "I've made my peace with the choices I've made, Evan. But that doesn't mean they were easy. It doesn't mean I don't have regrets, that I don't wonder every single day if I'm doing the right thing, if I'm being the best mother I can be to Chad."

I stare at her, shocked by the raw pain in her voice. "Molly, I..."

But she cuts me off, her words tumbling out in a rush. "You want to know about my marriage, Evan? You want to know why I'm so dang grateful for the life I have now? Because my ex was a liar and a cheat. Because he made me feel small, and stupid, and worthless. Because he left me with a mountain of debt and a broken heart and a little boy who cries himself to sleep at night wondering why his daddy doesn't love him anymore."

I feel like I've been punched in the gut; the air rushing out of my lungs. "Molly. I'm so sorry. I had no idea."

She wipes at her eyes, taking a shuddering breath. "I don't talk about it much," she says quietly. "It's not exactly a feel-good story. But my point is, I know what it's like to have your dreams shattered. To have to pick up the pieces and start over, even when it feels impossible. And I choose to be grateful, Evan. I choose to find joy in the life I have, because the alternative is giving up. And I will never, ever give up on my son."

I reach out, wanting to take her hand, to offer some kind of comfort. But she pulls away, wrapping her arms around herself like a shield.

"I think I should go," she says softly, her voice thick with tears.

My heart clenches, panic rising in my throat. "Molly, wait. Please. I didn't mean..."

But she's already turning away, her shoulders shaking with silent sobs as she disappears into the crowd.

I stand there, frozen, my mind reeling. What have I done? How could I have been so stupid, so selfish, so blind to the pain that Molly's been carrying all this time?

I think of all the moments we've shared, all the laughter and warmth and tentative hope. The way she makes me feel like I'm a part of something, like I belong.

And now, with a few thoughtless words, I may have ruined it all.

I close my eyes, fighting back the sting of tears. I don't know what to do, how to fix this. All I know is that the thought of losing Molly, of losing the one bright spot in my life, is more terrifying than anything I've ever faced.

I have to make this right. I have to show her how much she means to me, how sorry I am for making her doubt herself, doubt my feelings for her.

But as I stand there, lost and alone in the middle of the town square, the twinkling lights and joyful laughter suddenly hollow and false, I can't help but wonder if it's too late.

If I've already lost the one thing that matters most.

Eight

EVAN

The ceremony ends, the crowd dispersing in a flurry of chatter and laughter. But I barely notice, my mind still racing, my heart still aching with the weight of what I've done.

I wander through the streets, my feet carrying me aimlessly, my breath fogging in the cold night air. I pass the diner, the soon to be bookstore, and Hanks' department store. All the places that used to fill me with a sense of warmth, of belonging.

But now, they just feel empty. Meaningless. Like a life I no longer recognize, a future I'm no longer sure I want. Before long, I get in my truck and drive.

I end up at the farm, the familiar sight of the barn and the rows of trees doing little to calm the turmoil in my heart. I sit on the porch steps, my head in my hands, trying to make sense of the tangled mess of my thoughts.

"Evan? Is everything alright?"

I look up, startled by the gentle voice. Betty stands before me, her kind eyes filled with concern.

"Betty." I furrow my brow. "What are you doing here so late?"

"Oh, I forgot my scarf yesterday. Thought I'd pick it up on my way home."

I nod, my mind already back on Molly and the mess I made.

"Are you okay?" Betty asks with a kindness in her voice I don't deserve.

"I... I messed up. With Molly. I said some things, stupid things, and now... now I don't know if I can fix it."

She sits down beside me, the warmth of her presence comforting in the cold night air. "Tell me what happened."

And so I do. I pour out the whole story, the doubts, the fears, the cruel words I threw at Molly in a moment of selfishness and insecurity. Betty listens, her face soft with understanding.

"Evan," she says gently, when I've finally run out of words. "I want to ask you something, and I want you to answer honestly. Whose opinion do you value most in this world?"

I blink, taken aback by the question. "I... I don't know. I guess... I've always cared about what people think of me. What they expect of me."

Betty nods, her eyes wise and knowing. "But whose opinion matters most, Evan? When you picture your life, your future, whose approval do you need to be happy?"

And suddenly, I know. With a certainty that takes my

breath away. "My own," I whisper, my voice rough with emotion. "And Molly's."

I've only spent a few days with Molly, but I know there's something between us. I feel it. *Her* opinion matters to me.

She smiles, squeezing my hand. "Then that's your answer, Evan. That's what you fight for. Not the expectations of others, not some distant dream of a different life. But the love and happiness you've found, right here in Benton Falls."

Molly's face flashes in my mind, the hurt and betrayal in her eyes as she walked away. The way her voice broke, the tears she tried so hard to hide.

I think of Chad, of the way his face lights up every time he sees me, the trust and affection shining in his eyes. The way he looks at me like I'm some kind of hero, like I have all the answers.

Which I don't—but I have one—and for now that's enough.

"Thank you, Betty." I smile at this woman who seems to show up right when I need her. Like a surrogate mother. Maybe my mom sent her. "Thanks for listening."

"You're welcome." Betty gets up. "I better get going." She straightens her jacket and tucks her hands in her pockets. "And I guess you better, too."

I stand up, my knees aching from the cold, my heart pounding with a new sense of purpose. "Yeah, I do."

As I walk towards my truck, I find myself with a renewed sense of determination. Betty's words echo in my mind, a reminder of what truly matters. I glance back at the farmhouse, at the life I've built here, and feel a sense of gratitude.

With a deep breath, I climb into the driver's seat, the engine roaring to life beneath me. As I pull out onto the road, the farm disappearing in the rearview mirror; I feel a sense of clarity wash over me. I know what I have to do, what I need to say to make things right with Molly.

The miles slip away beneath my tires, the darkness of the night pressing in around me. But I barely notice; mind focused solely on the task at hand. I rehearse the words in my head, the apologies, the declarations of love and commitment. I pray it will be enough that Molly will see the sincerity in my eyes and the truth in my heart.

Before I know it, I'm turning onto her street, my heart hammering in my chest as I approach her house. But as I draw closer, a sense of unease prickles at the back of my neck. Something's not right.

I pull up to the curb, my eyes widening in shock at the scene before me. The front door hangs open, the wood splintered and broken. The windows are dark, jagged shards of glass littering the front lawn.

And then I hear it. The wailing of sirens, growing louder by the second. My stomach twists, fear and confusion warring within me.

"Molly," I whisper, my voice barely audible over the howling wind. "Chad."

I'm out of the truck in an instant, my feet pounding against the pavement as I race towards the house. I don't know what I'll find inside, what's happened here. But I know I have to find them to make sure they're safe.

I take the porch steps two at a time, my heart in my throat as I push open the ruined door. And then I freeze, my breath catching at the sight before me.

The house is in shambles, furniture overturned and belongings scattered across the floor. But there's no sign of Molly or Chad, no sign of where they might be or what's happened to them.

I move through the rooms, my eyes searching desperately for any clue, any hint of what's transpired here. But there's nothing, just an eerie stillness that sends chills down my spine.

As I stand in the middle of the chaos, the sirens drawing ever closer; I feel a wave of panic wash over me. Where are they? What's happened to them? And is it somehow my fault, a result of the harsh words and thoughtless actions that drove Molly away?

I don't know. I don't have any answers. All I know is that I have to find them to make sure they're okay. And to tell Molly how sorry I am, how much she means to me.

Before it's too late.

With a shaking hand, I pull out my phone, dialing Molly's number. It goes straight to voicemail, her cheerful greeting a stark contrast to the fear and uncertainty that grips my heart.

"Molly," I say, my voice rough with emotion. "It's Evan. I'm at your house and... and something's happened. Please, if you get this, call me back. I need to know you're okay. I need to know where you are."

I end the call, my hand clenching around the phone as I stare out at the empty street. The sirens are close now, the flashing lights of police cars illuminating the night.

But all I can think about is Molly and Chad, the two people who have come to mean more to me than anything in this world. And the sinking feeling in my gut that tells me something is very, very wrong.

I don't know what's going on, but I know one thing for certain.

I won't rest until I find them, until I know they're safe.

Nine

BETTY

I can't call it a night just yet—not after my talk with Evan. From a distance, I saw the hurt and frustration in Molly's eyes as she walked away from Evan at the tree lighting ceremony. My heart aches for them both, knowing how much they care for each other, and I wonder if Evan's apology will be enough for Molly. I need to know where things stand between them at the end of tonight so I can plan for tomorrow.

But as I make my way towards Molly's house, a sinking feeling settles in my gut. Something's not right. And when I turn the corner and see the police car parked outside, lights flashing like a warning sign, I know my instincts were spot on.

I rush towards the house, my human legs going as they can, and push past the small crowd of gathering onlookers. I can hear the whispers, the concern in their voices, but all I can think about is Molly and Chad. I have to make sure they're okay.

EVAN

Relief floods through me as I spot them emerging from the neighbor's house, Chad clinging to Molly's hand like a lifeline. They look shaken, but unharmed, and I send up a silent prayer of thanks to the big guy upstairs.

Evan's truck is parked in front of the police car, and I spot him as he leaps off the front porch, running towards Molly and Chad with open arms. For a moment, I think everything's going to be okay, that this scare will finally bring them together.

But as Evan tries to wrap Molly in a hug, she pulls away, her eyes guarded and her shoulders tense. "I'm fine, Evan," she says, her voice tight. "We're fine."

I can see the hurt flash across Evan's face, but he covers it quickly, nodding as he steps back. "I came to talk to you, to apologize, and then I saw the house." His voice is thick with emotion. "I was so worried."

Molly softens a bit at that, but there's still a wall up, a hesitation in her eyes. "Someone broke in while we were gone and the place is a disaster, but Chad and I are both fine." She exhales as she offers Chad a comforting smile, one that doesn't quite reach her eyes. "I appreciate you coming, Evan. Really. But it's been a long night, and we're exhausted. I think we just need some time to process everything."

A police officer approaches Molly and Evan. "I've filed a report, but I'll need you to come inside and get a detailed list of what's damaged or missing."

"Okay," Molly smiles, but the gesture is hollow. The poor girl. "Thanks Ren. I'll be inside in just a minute."

As they're talking, I notice a commotion coming from down the street. A group of neighbors, armed with cleaning supplies and determined expressions, marches towards Molly's house like a tiny army of goodwill.

"Molly, honey, we heard what happened," Mrs. Henderson from across the street calls out, her voice filled with concern. "We're here to help get your house back in order. Many hands make light work, you know."

Molly's eyes widen, her mouth falling open in surprise. "Oh, Mrs. Henderson, everyone... You don't have to do that. It's so late, and I'm sure you all have your own families to take care of."

But the neighbors are having none of it. They swarm around Molly, hugging her and patting her back, their voices rising in a chorus of support and encouragement.

"Nonsense, dear," Mr. Madson from next door, chimes in. "You're part of our family, too. And family takes care of each other, no matter what time it is or what else is going on."

Evan steps forward, his voice filled with admiration. "That's really kind of you."

Mrs. Henderson laughs, patting Evan on the arm. "Oh, honey, this is just what we do. When one of us is hurting, we all feel it. And we all pitch in to make it right."

As the neighbors bustle into the house, mops and brooms and trash bags in hand, I sidle up to Evan, nudging him with my elbow.

"Would you look at that," I murmur, nodding

towards the flurry of activity. "Benton Falls sure knows how to show up, huh?"

Evan shakes his head, a look of wonder and gratitude spreading across his face. "I've never seen anything like it," he says. "I mean, I knew this town was a pretty great place, but this... This is something else entirely."

I smile, feeling a swell of pride and affection for this little community that's found its way into my heart so quickly. "That's the magic of a small town, kiddo. When the chips are down, they circle the wagons and take care of their own. It's a beautiful thing to see."

We watch in silence for a moment, marveling at the way the neighbors work together, their laughter and chatter filling the night air. But then I catch a snippet of conversation that makes my heart clench.

"Molly, honey, I'm so sorry," Mrs. Larson says, her voice filled with sympathy. "I can't believe they took all the Christmas presents. After everything you've been through this year..."

Molly swallows hard, her eyes glistening with unshed tears. "It's okay," she says, her voice wavering slightly. "They're just things. What matters is that Chad and I are safe. We can always replace the presents."

But I can see the pain in her eyes, the weariness and disappointment that she's trying so hard to hide. And I know that for a single mom like Molly, those presents were more than just things. They were a symbol of love and sacrifice, of the endless hours she's worked to make sure her son has a magical Christmas, no matter what.

I turn to Evan, my heart aching for this little family

that's come to mean so much to me. "We have to do something," I whisper, my voice fierce with determination. "We can't let them go without Christmas, not after everything they've been through."

Evan nods, his jaw set with resolve. "I know. And we won't. I promise you, Betty, I'm going to make this right. Whatever it takes, I'm going to give Molly and Chad the Christmas they deserve."

I feel tears prick at the corners of my eyes, pride and love and the purest sense of rightness washing over me. He's grown so much over the past few days.

I smile, patting his hand as I stand up. "I think that sounds perfect."

Evan looks at me, a flicker of understanding in his eyes. "You know, Betty, sometimes I feel like you're more than just a kind neighbor. It's like you've got this... I don't know, this wisdom, this way of seeing things that's just..." He shakes his head, chuckling softly. "Listen to me, getting all sentimental. Must be the Christmas spirit getting to my head."

I laugh, giving him a playful nudge. "Oh, hush now. You're not going soft on me, are you, Evan Lawson?"

He grins, that boyish charm shining through. "Wouldn't dream of it, Betty. You'd never let me hear the end of it."

"Darn right, I wouldn't," I agree, feeling a rush of affection for this stubborn, big-hearted human who's wormed his way into my soul. "Someone's got to keep you on your toes, kid."

And with a final wink and a nod, I turn to go, feeling

the familiar tug of the celestial realm calling me home. But even as the shimmering threads of heaven welcome me back into their embrace, I can't stop thinking about Molly and Evan, about the incredible journey they're on and the beautiful future that awaits them.

Ten

EVAN

The scent of freshly baked apple pie and hot rolls wafts through the air as I step into Violet's Diner, the warmth of the cozy eatery enveloping me like a comforting hug. It's been a week since the break-in at Molly's house, and though the community has rallied around her, I can't shake the feeling that I'm continuing to let her down somehow.

I slide into my usual booth, the red vinyl creaking beneath me. The diner is buzzing with activity, locals chatting over steaming mugs of coffee and plates piled high with hearty comfort food. But as I scan the room, my eyes searching for Molly, I feel a knot of anxiety tighten in my stomach.

Things have been strained between us since our argument at the tree lighting ceremony and she hasn't been to work on the farm. I know I spoke out of turn, let my own frustrations and fears get the best of me. But seeing

Molly so upset, so hurt by my careless words... it's been eating away at me ever since.

I'm lost in thought, absently fiddling with the salt shaker, when a familiar voice jolts me back to the present.

"Evan? What can I get for you tonight?"

I look up to see Molly standing beside the booth, her order pad in hand. She looks tired, dark circles beneath her hazel eyes, but there's still a warmth in her smile that makes my heart skip a beat.

"Hey, Molly," I say gently, trying to gauge her mood. "I'll just have the usual, thanks."

She nods, jotting down my order. But as she turns to leave, I reach out, my hand brushing against her arm.

"Wait, Molly... can we talk for a minute?"

She hesitates, her gaze flickering to the bustling diner around us. But then she sighs, sliding into the booth across from me.

"Sure, Evan. What's on your mind?"

I take a deep breath, trying to find the right words. "I wanted to apologize, Molly. For the way I acted at the tree lighting ceremony, for the things I said. I was out of line, and I'm sorry."

Molly's eyes soften, a flicker of understanding crossing her face. "I appreciate that, Evan. And I'm sorry, too. I didn't handle that well."

I shake my head, reaching across the table to take her hand in mine. "You have nothing to apologize for Molly and again, I'm so sorry about your house. If there's anything I can do..."

She smiles, her fingers tightening around mine.

"You've already done more than enough." Her eyes are brimming with emotion. "I know it was you who paid for the security system to be installed, not to mention the anonymous gift card to 'Hanks' Department Store'."

My brow furrows as my face heats. "That was supposed to be a secret." I huff and cross my arms over my chest. "And it was purely selfish. I feel a lot better knowing you and Chad are safe."

We sit there for a moment, lost in each other's eyes, the rest of the world fading away. But then Molly clears her throat, pulling her hand back as she remembers where we are.

"I should probably get back to work," she says, a hint of regret in her voice. "But thank you, Evan. For everything."

I nod, watching as she slides out of the booth and heads back to the kitchen. But before she disappears behind the swinging door, I call out to her.

"Hey, Molly? Your wreath-making job at the farm... it's still open whenever you're ready to come back. We miss having you around."

She pauses, a surprised smile tugging at her lips. "Thanks, Evan. I'll keep that in mind."

As she vanishes into the kitchen, I feel a weight lift off my shoulders. It's not much, but it's a start. A step towards mending the rift between us, towards finding our way back to the easy camaraderie and budding connection we'd been building before everything went sideways.

EVAN

I'm just digging into my meatloaf when a familiar voice pipes up from beside the booth.

"Hi, Mr. Evan."

I look up to see Chad grinning at me, his sandy hair tousled and his cheeks flushed from the cold.

"Hey there, buddy." I say, setting down my fork. "What brings you here tonight?"

"Mom had to work, so I'm hanging out until she's done," he explains, sliding into the booth across from me. "Are you going to the Community Caroling Night tonight?"

I blink, surprised by the question. "The what now?"

"The singing night." Chad says, his eyes sparkling with excitement. "It's this big thing where the whole town gets together in the square and sings Christmas songs. There's hot cocoa and cookies and everything. Mom's getting off early so we can go."

I chuckle, charmed by his enthusiasm. "That sounds pretty great. But I don't know, buddy. I'm not much of a singer."

Chad's face falls, his bottom lip jutting out in a pout. "But it won't be the same without you, Mr. Evan. Please say you'll come?"

I hesitate, glancing towards the kitchen where Molly is bustling about. "I don't know, Chad. I'm not sure if your mom would want me there."

But Chad is undeterred, his eyes wide and pleading. "She will want you to come. You are best friends, remember? She likes you, Mr. Evan. I can tell."

I feel a flush creep up my neck, my heart stuttering in my chest. "She does, huh?"

Chad nods vigorously, his little face serious. "Yep. And I like you, too. You make her smile, even when she's sad."

I swallow hard, a lump rising in my throat. "I like your mom a lot, too, Chad. And you. I hope you know that."

He beams at me, his smile brighter than the twinkling Christmas lights outside. "I know. So you'll come to the caroling thing? Please?"

I sigh, unable to resist the hopeful look on his face. "Alright, buddy. You win. I'll be there."

Chad lets out a whoop of joy, fist-pumping the air. "Yes!"

I can't stop myself from laughing, his excitement contagious. And as I watch him scamper off to tell Molly the good news, I feel a flicker of something warm and bright kindling in my chest. I marvel at his innocent joy. Even after having his home broken into, and his gifts stolen, he still sees the good, feels the excitement of the season, and smiles through it all.

Maybe Chad is right. Maybe this will be the best Christmas ever, not because of the presents or the decorations, but because of the people I get to spend it with. The people who are starting to feel more and more like family with each passing day.

EVAN

Later that night, I find myself standing in the middle of the town square, surrounded by what seems like the entire population of Benton Falls. The air is frosty and cold, the scent of marshmallows and spiced apples permeating from the vendors selling hot cocoa and cider.

I tug at the collar of my coat, feeling oddly nervous as I scan the crowd for Molly and Chad. We'd agreed to meet here, but as the minutes tick by and the caroling gets underway, I worry that maybe they've changed their minds.

But then I see them, weaving their way through the throng of people, Chad's hand clasped tightly in Molly's. She looks beautiful, her chestnut hair spilling out from beneath a knit hat, her cheeks flushed from the cold. And when she spots me, her face lighting up in a smile that makes my heart skip a beat; I feel like the luckiest man in the world.

"Evan, hi," she says, a little breathless as they reach me. "Sorry we're late. Someone had to hurry and finish their homework before we could leave."

She shoots Chad a mock-stern look, but he just grins up at her, unrepentant.

"I'm here now, aren't I?" he says, bouncing on his toes. "And look, Mr. Evan is here, too. Just like he promised."

I chuckle, ruffling Chad's hair. "I wouldn't miss it for the world, buddy. Not when I've got you to keep me in line."

Molly rolls her eyes, but there's a warmth in her gaze

that makes me feel like I'm standing in a patch of sunlight, even in the middle of the winter night.

"Come on, you two," she says, herding us towards the group of carolers. "Let's go make some joyful noise."

As we join the crowd, the sounds of "Deck the Halls" ringing out into the frosty air, I find myself marveling at the sense of community, of belonging that washes over me. Everywhere I look, people are smiling and laughing, their faces aglow with the spirit of the season.

And as I glance around, my gaze landing on the familiar faces of my neighbors, my customers, the people who have become such an integral part of my life here in Benton Falls, I feel a sudden rush of gratitude, of appreciation for the beauty and simplicity of this place.

Maybe the adventure I've been searching for has been right here in front of me, waiting to be discovered in the laughter of a child, the touch of a woman's hand, the quiet magic of a Christmas spent with the people I love.

As the caroling continues, the voices of young and old blending together in perfect harmony, I let myself get lost in the music, in the moment. And as I do, I feel a sense of peace settling over me, a rightness that I haven't felt in longer than I can remember.

I reach out, taking Molly's hand in mine, feeling the warmth of her fingers even through our gloves, and I know that I'm finally ready to take that leap, to open my heart to the possibilities of the future.

She looks up at me, her bright eyes shining beneath a fringe of dark lashes, and smiles. I'm so lost in my thoughts, in the swelling emotions that fill my chest, that

I almost don't notice when the carol comes to an end, the final notes lingering in the air.

Molly turns to me. "That was beautiful," she murmurs, her voice soft and filled with wonder. "I can't remember the last time I felt so... so..."

"Peaceful," I finish for her, understanding flickering between us like a flame. "Like everything is exactly as it should be."

She nods, a smile playing at the corners of her mouth. "Yes. Exactly."

We stand there for a moment, lost in each other's gaze, the rest of the world fading away. But then Chad is tugging at my sleeve, his little face eager.

"Mr. Evan, can we go get some hot cocoa now? I'm freezing."

I laugh, the spell broken, but the warmth still glowing in my chest. "Of course, buddy. Lead the way."

As we make our way towards the cocoa stand, weaving through the crowds of carolers and onlookers, I catch a glimpse of a familiar face in the throng. Betty, bundled up in a bright red coat, her eyes twinkling with a secret sort of joy as she watches us.

For a moment, I swear I can feel the weight of her gaze, the unspoken encouragement and understanding that passes between us like a current. And then she's gone, disappearing into the crowd as quickly as she appeared.

But the warmth of her presence lingers, a reminder of the countless little moments of guidance and support she's offered me over the past couple of weeks. The way

Betty always seems to show up just when I need her most, with a kind word or a gentle nudge in the right direction.

I don't know how she does it, how she always seems to know exactly what I need to hear. But as I stand in line for cocoa, Chad chattering away at my side and Molly's hand still clasped in mine, I feel a rush of gratitude for her friendship, for the quiet strength and wisdom—she's kind of like my own Christmas angel.

As we sip our cocoa, the rich, velvety sweetness chasing away the chill, I let myself get lost in the simple pleasure of the moment. The twinkling lights of the Christmas tree, the soft murmur of conversation, the way Molly's shoulder brushes against mine as we stand huddled together against the cold.

It's perfect. All of it. The cocoa, the company, the sheer magic of this night. I turn to Molly, my heart hammering in my chest as I take a deep breath, gathering my courage.

"Molly," I begin, my voice soft but filled with determination. "There's something I've been wanting to ask you."

She looks up at me, her eyes searching mine, a flicker of curiosity and hope dancing in their hazel depths. "What is it, Evan?"

I reach out, taking her hand in mine, marveling at the way our fingers intertwine, like two halves of a whole, finally coming together.

"Molly, would you like to go on a date with me? A real date, just the two of us, where we can talk and laugh and get to know each other with no distractions or interruptions?" I smile as I glance at her son, who's wearing a chocolate mustache. "Not that I don't love spending time with Chad, but jus the two of us sounds nice."

A smile blooms across her face, radiant and beautiful. "Just the two of us would be really nice," she says, her voice filled with warmth and affection.

I grin, feeling like I could float away on the sheer happiness that bubbles up inside me. "Great. That's... that's fantastic. How about Saturday? Can you get work off that night at the diner? I could pick you up at six, and we could go to Casa Rameriez?"

"I would love that," Molly says, her eyes sparkling with anticipation. "But how about tomorrow night? I'm on the day shift tomorrow, and I'm sure Saturday will be a busy day on the farm."

"That works too," I grin. The sooner the better for me.

"And I don't work Saturday, so Chad and I can help all day at the farm, if you want us to."

"Yes, please." I squeeze her fingers. "I can't think of anything better."

We stand there for a moment longer, our hands still clasped together, the rest of the world fading away until there is nothing but the three of us, the snowflakes swirling around us like a benediction.

As I look into Molly's eyes, as I see the hope and the promise and the sheer, unbridled potential shining back at me, and I think Chad is right—this is going to be the best Christmas ever.

Eleven

EVAN

I glance at my watch for the hundredth time, my leg bouncing nervously as I sit on the edge of my bed. 5:45 PM. In just fifteen minutes, I'll be picking up Molly for our first real date, and I'm equal parts excited and terrified. I'm also grateful Paul and Seth agreed to manage the farm tonight. I'll remember their kindness when it's time for a Christmas bonus.

Standing up, I check my reflection in the mirror one last time, running my fingers over stubble free face. I've traded in my usual flannel and work boots for a nice blue button-down and a pair of dark jeans. I even broke out the good leather boots, the ones I usually save for special occasions. And let's be real, a date with Molly? Definitely qualifies as special.

Grabbing my coat and keys, I head out to my truck with a spring in my step. The air is brisk, with a woodsy scent drifting on the breeze. As I drive through the quiet streets of Benton Falls, I can't stop myself from thinking about how much has changed in the past couple of weeks.

Not too long ago, I was just going through the motions, working on the farm and dreaming of a life somewhere else. But then Molly and Chad came along, and suddenly, everything was different. Suddenly, I had a reason to stick around, to put down roots and build something real.

I pull up outside Molly's house, taking a deep breath before I climb out of the truck. I walk up to the front door, my heart pounding in my chest as I knock. I hear footsteps, and then the door swings open, revealing Molly.

And dang, she looks incredible.

Her chestnut hair is falling in soft waves around her face, and she's wearing this camel colored sweater dress that hugs her curves in all the right places. She's got on a pair of black leggings and knee-high boots, and I swear, her legs go on for miles.

"Wow," I breathe, trying to keep my jaw from hitting the floor. "You look amazing."

Molly blushes, a small smile tugging at her lips. "Thanks. You clean up pretty well yourself." Her fingers brush along my smooth jawline as her smile widens. "I like it."

"Good," I grin, offering her my arm. "Shall we?"

She nods, grabbing her coat and purse. "Let's go. I just dropped Chad off at Mrs. Henderson's. He's been begging to play with her cat all week."

I chuckle as I help her into the truck. "That kid sure loves animals."

"He really does," Molly agrees, buckling her seatbelt. "I think it's sweet. He's got such a big heart."

I nod, pulling out onto the road. "Just like his mom."

Molly ducks her head, but I can see the smile on her face. "You're quite the charmer, aren't you, Evan Lawson?"

"Only with you," I reply, giving her a wink. "I guess you just bring out the best in me."

She laughs, the sound warming me from the inside out. "Well, I could say the same about you. I haven't felt this happy, this excited about the future, in a long time."

I reach over, taking her hand in mine. "Me neither, Molly. You and Chad... you've given me something to look forward to. It means a lot to me. *You* mean a lot to me."

Molly bites her lip and I'm worried I've said too much, but when I look into her eyes, all I see is joy shining back at me.

We chat easily as I drive, talking about our days and swapping stories. It's comfortable, natural, like we've been doing this for years instead of just a few short weeks.

When we pull up to the rear entrance of Casa Ramirez, the parking lot is packed. I guess everyone in town had the same idea for date night. We make our way inside; the hostess leading us to a cozy table in the corner.

As we sit down, I take a moment to just look at Molly, to drink in the sight of her in the soft glow of the pendant lights. She's radiant, her skin smooth and golden, her eyes bright and warm. I feel like the luckiest guy in the world, getting to be here with her.

"I'm really glad we're doing this," I say, reaching across the table to take her hand. "I've been looking forward to tonight ever since last night."

Molly smiles, her fingers lacing with mine. "Me too. I kept catching myself daydreaming at work, counting down the hours until I could see you again."

I grin, feeling a rush of warmth in my chest. "Well, now you've got me for the whole night. Think you can handle it?"

She laughs, giving my hand a squeeze. "Oh, I think I'm up for the challenge. Bring it on, Lawson."

We order a bunch of food—sizzling fajitas, cheesy enchiladas, tangy salsa—and dig in, talking and laughing between bites. Molly tells me about the crazy customers she had at the diner today, and I share some stories about the families who came to the farm looking for the perfect Christmas tree.

"I love watching you with the kids," Molly says, her eyes soft. "You're so good with them, so patient and kind. It's one of the things I admire most about you."

I feel my cheeks heat at the compliment. "Thanks, Molly. That means a lot coming from you. Seeing the way you are with Chad, the love and devotion you have for him... it's incredible. He's lucky to have you."

"We're lucky to have each other," she says, her voice catching a little. "And now, we're pretty lucky to have you, too."

I lift her hand to my lips, pressing a soft kiss to her knuckles. "Trust me, Molly, I'm the lucky one."

Molly's eyes shine with emotion, and she leans across the table, her face inches from mine. "Evan, I... I know we haven't known each other long, but this feels right... right?"

I swallow hard, my heart pounding in my chest. "Yeah, it feels right."

And then I'm leaning in, my hand coming up to cup her cheek, my thumb brushing over the soft skin. Molly's eyes flutter closed, and I close the distance between us, pressing my lips to hers in a gentle kiss.

It's perfect. Molly's lips are soft and sweet, and she sighs into the kiss as I savor the feel of her mouth on mine. My heart thumps in my chest, reaffirming how amazing this moment is.

When we break apart, we're both breathless and grinning like idiots. "Wow," I murmur, resting my forehead against hers. "That was..."

"Amazing," Molly finishes, her eyes sparkling with joy. "Definitely worth repeating."

I laugh, stealing another quick kiss. "Definitely. But maybe we should wait until we're not in the middle of a crowded restaurant. Don't want to give the other diners a show."

Molly giggles, sitting back in her chair. "Good point. We should probably head out, anyway. I told Mrs. Henderson I'd pick up Chad by ten."

I nod, signaling for the check. As we walk out to the truck, I can't keep the stupid grin off my face. I just kissed

Molly Bennett. I just had the best first date of my life. And from the way she's smiling at me, I think she feels the same way.

Driving home, the conversation flows easily between us. When I pull up outside her house, I hop out to open her door, walking her up to the front porch.

"I had an incredible time tonight," Molly says, her eyes locked on mine. "Thank you for making it so special."

I shake my head, taking her hands in mine. "I'm the one who should be thanking you, Molly. For giving me another chance, for being so amazing... for everything."

She smiles, leaning in to press a soft kiss to my lips. "You're pretty amazing yourself," she whispers, her breath warm against my lips.

And then we're kissing again, our bodies melting together as if they were made for each other. Molly's arms wind around my neck, her fingers threading through my hair as she pulls me closer. I wrap my arms around her waist, savoring the feel of her curves pressed against me.

The kiss is deep and passionate, filled with all the pent-up desire and affection we've been holding back all night. Molly's lips are soft and pliant beneath mine, her tongue tangling with my own in a dance that sets my blood on fire.

I lose track of time, lost in the taste and feel of her, in the little sighs and moans that escape her throat. It's only when my lungs burn that we finally pull back, both of us flushed and panting.

"Not that's how you say goodbye," Molly says breathlessly, her eyes dark and heavy-lidded.

I nod, reluctantly loosening my hold on her. "Not goodbye, just goodnight."

Suddenly, I'm very aware of how much this woman means to me.

Molly laughs, pressing one last soft kiss to my lips before stepping back. "Just goodnight then. I'll see you soon?"

"Count on it," I reply, my heart soaring at the promise in her words. "Sweet dreams, Molly."

She smiles, and then she's gone, fading into the warmth and light of her home. I stand there for a moment, grinning like a fool, before heading back to my truck.

As I drive away, my mind replays every moment of the night, from the laughter and conversation to the toe-curling kisses on Molly's front porch. And I know, with a certainty that thrills me to my core, that this is just the beginning of something truly special.

I can't wait to see what tomorrow brings.

Twelve

BETTY

As my feet touch the ground, the frosty winter air filling my lungs, I'm in awe of the transformation that has taken place in Evan Lawson's life over the past couple of weeks. The farm, once a source of resentment and restlessness, now seems to hum with a newfound sense of purpose and possibility, the rows of Christmas trees standing tall and proud like sentinels of hope.

And at the center of it all, like a shining beacon, is the blossoming love between Evan and Molly, the tentative yet powerful connection that has reshaped both of their lives in ways they never could have imagined.

The day after their official first date, I find Evan and Molly working together at the Christmas tree farm, their faces aglow with the joy and excitement of their budding romance. Molly sits at a large wooden table in the barn, her nimble fingers weaving fragrant evergreen boughs into beautiful wreaths. She hums softly to herself as she works, a contented smile playing at the corners of her mouth.

Evan, meanwhile, is out in the fields with Chad, teaching the boy how to properly care for the trees and select the best ones for customers. I watch as Chad listens intently to Evan's instructions, his young face alight with eagerness and admiration. It's clear that he looks up to Evan, sees him as a mentor and a father figure, and the bond between them warms my heart.

As the day wears on, I observe the easy camaraderie and affection that flows between Evan and Molly, the way they steal glances at each other when they think no one is looking, the gentle touches and soft laughter that speak of a deep and growing connection.

I watch as they work side by side, stringing lights and hanging ornaments, their laughter and easy banter drifting on the cool winter air. Evan's eyes sparkle with a warmth and contentment I've never seen before, his smile genuine and unguarded as he steals glances at Molly when he thinks she's not looking.

And Molly... oh, the change in her is nothing short of miraculous. The weariness that once seemed to weigh on her shoulders has lifted, replaced by a lightness, a radiance, that speaks of a heart slowly learning to trust and hope and believe in the possibility of joy once more.

It's a beautiful thing to witness, this delicate dance of two souls finding their way to each other, learning to open up and let love in. And as I watch them, I feel a swell of pride and gratitude rising in my chest, a sense of purpose and fulfillment that goes beyond anything I ever experienced in my earthly life.

This, right here, is what it means to be a guardian angel. To guide and nurture and support these precious human lives, to help them discover the strength and resilience and boundless capacity for love that lies within them.

And yet, even as I revel in the progress Evan and Molly have made, in the beautiful future that seems to stretch out before them, I can't shake the feeling that their journey is far from over.

As if sensing my unease, Henry appears beside me, his wise eyes twinkling with understanding and compassion. "You're doing well, Betty," he says, laying a comforting hand on my shoulder. "Evan and Molly have come so far, and it's in no small part thanks to your guidance and support."

I nod, feeling a flush of warmth at his praise. "I just want them to be happy, Henry. To find the love and joy and sense of belonging that they both deserve."

He smiles, his gaze drifting to where Evan and Molly are now engaged in a playful snowball fight, their laughter ringing out across the farm. "And they will, my dear. But remember, the path to true happiness is rarely a straight or easy one. There will be twists and turns, moments of darkness and doubt. It's our job to be there for them, to offer light and hope and guidance when they need it most."

I sigh, knowing he's right. "I just wish I could protect them from all the pain and heartache that might still lie ahead. I wish I could wave a magic wand and make everything perfect for them."

Henry chuckles, shaking his head. "Ah, but where would be the growth in that? The learning, the transformation, the sheer beauty of the human spirit rising to meet its challenges and emerge stronger and wiser and more deeply connected to the love that surrounds us all?"

I nod, understanding the truth of his words even as my heart aches for the struggles I know Evan and Molly may still face. "You're right, of course. It's just hard sometimes, watching them stumble and fall, knowing I can't always catch them or cushion the blow."

"But that's the beauty of free will, isn't it?" Henry muses, his eyes sparkling with a mix of mischief and profound wisdom. "The power of choice, the freedom to create our own paths and learn from our own mistakes. It's what makes the human experience so rich and complex and utterly miraculous."

I smile, feeling a rush of affection for this wise and humble soul who has been my mentor and guide throughout this incredible journey. "Thank you, Henry. For always knowing just what to say to put things in perspective."

He winks, patting my hand. "That's what I'm here for, my dear. To offer a little angelic insight and a lot of unwavering faith in the unfolding plan."

With a final squeeze of my shoulder, he vanishes, leaving me alone once more to watch over my charges, to witness the next chapter of their story as it unfolds.

And as the sun sets over the farm, casting a golden

glow over the snow-covered fields, I feel a sense of peace and rightness settle over me, a deep knowing that Evan and Molly are exactly where they're meant to be, on the cusp of a beautiful and fulfilling future together.

I watch as Chad makes his way to Evan and Molly. Evan helps Molly load the finished wreaths into the back of his truck, his strong hands gentle and protective as he guides her. And when they pause for a moment, their eyes meeting in a gaze filled with tenderness and promise, I feel a swell of optimism and hope rising in my chest.

With a final glance at the happy couple, I feel a sense of contentment and joy wash over me. They've found each other, and their love is strong and true.

What could possibly go wrong?

Thirteen

EVAN

Saturday evening, the sun dips below the horizon as I finish up the last of the day's chores on the farm. My muscles ache with the satisfying exhaustion that comes from a hard day's work, and I find myself smiling as I look out over the rows of trees, their branches heavy with the first dusting of winter snow.

Two weeks until Christmas and it's been a busy day, with customers coming in droves to pick out their perfect Christmas trees. Even in the midst of the chaos, I've found myself stealing glances at Molly as she works beside me, her cheeks flushed from the cold and her eyes sparkling with joy.

Every time our eyes meet, every time our hands brush as we pass a wreath or a string of lights, I feel a flutter in my chest. It's a warmth that has nothing to do with the exertion of the day, and everything to do with the growing connection between us.

As I head back to the barn to put away my tools, I

wave at Paul and Seth as they get into their trucks and catch sight of Chad, his little face alight with excitement as he runs towards me, his boots kicking up puffs of snow.

"Evan." he calls out, his voice breathless with anticipation. "Can we go on the sleigh ride now? Please, please, please?"

I chuckle, scooping him up and tossing him over my shoulder like a sack of potatoes. "I don't know, buddy. Have you been a good boy today?"

He giggles, squirming in my grasp. "I've been the best. I helped Mom with the wreaths and everything."

I set him down, ruffling his sandy hair with affection. "Well, in that case, I think a sleigh ride is definitely in order. Why don't you go find your mom and tell her to bundle up? I'll get the horses ready."

Chad whoops with joy and takes off like a shot towards the barn, his little legs pumping as he disappears inside. I watch him go, feeling a swell of warmth in my chest at his enthusiasm.

In the few short weeks since Molly and Chad came into my life, they've become a bright spot in my days. As I make my way to the stables to harness up the horses, I can't help but marvel at how quickly they've worked their way into my heart.

It's not just the big things, like the way Molly's smile makes my pulse race or the way Chad's laughter fills the empty spaces around the farm. It's the little things too, the quiet moments of connection that have formed between us.

As I lead the horses out of the stable, their breath puffing in the frosty air, I catch sight of Molly and Chad making their way towards me, bundled up in coats and scarves and hats. Molly's cheeks are red from the cold, her eyes bright with anticipation, and I feel my heart skip a beat at the sight of her.

"Ready for an adventure?" I ask as they reach me, my voice warm with affection.

Molly smiles up at me, her gloved hand brushing against mine. "Absolutely. This is so exciting."

Chad's eyes widen when he looks at the horses. "Wow! They're huge. What are their names?"

"The big grey is Jumbo, and the black one is Doc." I smile and run my hand along Jumbo's neck. "They love to go in the snow."

I help Molly and Chad into the sleigh, tucking a thick wool blanket around their laps to ward off the chill. Chad is practically vibrating with excitement, his little mittened hands gripping the sides of the sleigh as he peers out at the snow-covered fields.

"Can we go fast, Evan?" he asks, his voice high and eager. "Like, really, really fast?"

I chuckle, climbing into the driver's seat and taking up the reins. "We'll see, buddy. Safety first, remember?"

As we set off, the horses' hooves kicking up sprays of powdery snow, I can't resist the urge to give Chad a little thrill. I snap the reins, urging the horses into a brisk trot, and the sleigh surges forward, the runners cutting through the snow like a knife through butter.

Chad lets out a whoop of joy, his laughter ringing

out across the fields, and I feel Molly's hand grip the side of the sleigh, her body leaning slightly into mine as we fly over the snow.

It's exhilarating, the cold wind whipping at our faces, the world blurring past in a swirl of white and gray. But even more than the physical thrill, it's the feeling of shared joy and wonder that makes my heart soar.

I glance over at Molly, taking in the flush of her cheeks, the sparkle of her eyes, the way her hair whips out behind her like a banner in the wind. She looks so alive, so vibrant, that it takes my breath away.

"Having fun?" I ask, my voice raised to be heard over the pounding of the horses' hooves.

She turns to me; her smile brighter than the sun on the snow. "The best," she says, her voice filled with laughter and happiness. "I feel like I'm flying."

"You are," I tell her, my own smile stretching wide across my face. "We all are."

As we settle into a steady rhythm, the initial excitement gives way to a comfortable companionship. Chad nestles between us, his eyes wide as he takes in the winter wonderland around us.

"So, Molly," I begin, curiosity getting the better of me, "what made you decide to stay in Benton Falls?"

Molly turns her head, her expression thoughtful. "I like the town and even after my ex-husband left, I couldn't imagine going anywhere else." Her eyes scanning the snow-covered fields and forests around us. "It's beautiful here as well. The farm is so peaceful."

"It can be lonely too," I admit, surprising myself with

my honesty. "But lately... well, it's been nice having you and Chad around."

Molly's cheeks, already pink from the cold, seem to flush a shade deeper. "We've loved being here. You've made us feel so welcome."

There's a moment of charged silence, broken by Chad's excited voice. "Look, Mommy. A deer."

We all turn to see a doe and her fawn at the edge of the forest, their delicate forms silhouetted against the snow.

"Oh, wow," Molly breathes, her hand unconsciously reaching for mine beneath the blanket. I give her fingers a gentle squeeze, sharing in the wonder of the moment.

As the deer bound away into the forest, Chad turns to me, his eyes shining. "Evan, do you see deer here all the time?"

I chuckle, ruffling his hair. "Pretty often, buddy. Maybe if you and your mom keep visiting, we can go on a nature walk sometime. I could show you all the best spots for wildlife watching."

"Can we, Mom? Please?" Chad looks at Molly with pleading eyes.

Molly laughs, shooting me a warm glance. "I think that sounds lovely. We'll have to take Evan up on that offer."

As we continue our ride, the conversation flows easily between us. We talk about our favorite Christmas traditions, our hopes for the new year, and our shared love of hot chocolate on cold winter nights. It's comfortable and exciting all at once, like we're old friends discovering new depths to our relationship.

The sky darkens to a velvety black studded with stars; the moon casting a silvery glow over the snow. Chad's chatter has faded to a sleepy murmur, his head resting against Molly's shoulder as he drifts off to sleep.

Molly and I sit in comfortable silence, our hands now resting close beneath the blanket, our breath mingling in the frosty air. It's peaceful, a moment of quiet connection that feels special, even if we're still getting to know each other.

"Evan?" Molly's voice is soft, almost hesitant, as if she's afraid to break the spell.

"Yeah?" I turn to look at her, my heart skipping a beat at the warmth in her eyes.

"I just wanted to say thank you," she murmurs, her fingers brushing against mine. "For today, for everything. It's been magical."

I swallow hard, my throat suddenly tight with emotion. "I'm glad you've enjoyed it. Having you and Chad here... it's made the farm feel alive in a way it hasn't in years."

She smiles, her eyes glistening in the moonlight. "We've loved being here, too. It feels like... I don't know, like we've found something special."

I nod, my gaze holding hers with an intensity that surprises even me. "I feel the same way. I'm really glad you gave constructing wreaths a chance."

She chuckles as I grin and then we share a moment of silent understanding, both aware of the potential growing between us, but neither quite ready to put it into words.

As we turn back towards the farm, the lights twinkling in the distance, I feel a smile spreading across my face, a warmth and contentment that fills me from head to toe.

When we pull up to the barn, I hop down from the sleigh and help Molly disembark. Chad is fast asleep, his little face peaceful in the moonlight.

"I can carry him to your car," I offer quietly, not wanting to wake the sleeping boy.

Molly nods gratefully. "That would be wonderful, thank you."

I gently lift Chad from the sleigh, cradling him against my chest as we make our way towards Molly's car. His weight is warm and solid in my arms, and I'm struck by how natural it feels, how right.

As we reach the vehicle, Molly opens the back door, and I carefully settle Chad into his booster seat, making sure not to wake him. Once he's secure, I step back, suddenly aware of how close Molly and I are standing.

"Thank you for today," Molly says, her eyes meeting mine in the dim light. "It was perfect."

I smile as palpable energy flows between us. "I'm glad. Maybe we could do it again sometime?"

She nods, a shy smile playing at her lips. "I'd like that."

For a moment, we stand there, a current of unspoken possibilities between us. I take my chance and give her a quick kiss. Even with Chad asleep, I know to be cautious.

Her mouth is still the best thing I've ever tasted, and the kiss only leaves me wanting more. Then, with a gentle squeeze of my arm, Molly steps back.

"Goodnight, Evan," she says. "See you tomorrow?"

I nod, my voice a bit husky as I reply, "Goodnight, Molly. Drive safe."

As I watch her car pull away, the taillights fading into the night, I'm filled with a sense of anticipation, of hope. Whatever is growing between us, it feels real and precious, and I can't wait to see where it might lead.

With a contented sigh, I turn back towards the farmhouse, the memory of the sleigh ride and Molly's smile warming me even on the cold winter night.

Fourteen

EVAN

The December air nips at my cheeks as I step out of my truck, the gravel crunching beneath my boots. The sun, a pale disk in the winter sky, casts long shadows across the church parking lot. I take a deep breath, inhaling the scent of pine and wood smoke that seems to permeate everything in Benton Falls during the holiday season.

As I adjust my collar, smoothing down the unfamiliar stiffness of my Sunday best, I catch sight of Molly's car pulling into the lot and my heart does a little skip. It's been happening more and more lately, this involuntary reaction to her presence. Like my body knows she's near before my mind has even registered it.

I watch as she parks and helps Chad out of the backseat. Even from here, I can see the way her chestnut hair catches the sunlight, the graceful curve of her neck as she bends to adjust Chad's coat. She's wearing a gold sweater dress that hugs her slender figure, and I find myself mesmerized by the way she moves, elegant and purposeful all at once.

Chad spots me first, his face lighting up with that infectious grin of his. "Evan!" he calls out, waving enthusiastically. "We're here."

I smile back, raising my hand in greeting. "I see that, buddy. Right on time, too."

As they make their way over, I feel a sense of rightness settle over me. It's a feeling that's been growing stronger with each day Molly spends at the farm, making wreaths and bringing life back to the place in a way I never expected.

"Good morning," Molly says as they reach me, her hazel eyes warm with affection. "I hope we didn't keep you waiting."

"Not at all," I assure her, resisting the urge to reach out and tuck a stray strand of hair behind her ear. "I just got here myself."

Chad, bouncing on his toes with barely contained energy, looks up at me with wide eyes. "Is this your church, Evan? Do you come here every Sunday?"

I chuckle, ruffling his sandy hair. "It sure is, buddy. And I'll admit I haven't been here as often as I should."

Molly gives me a knowing smile. "Well, we're glad you could make it today. It means a lot to have you here with us."

Her words send a warmth spreading through my chest, and I find myself standing a little straighter. "I wouldn't miss it," I tell her softly, meaning every word.

As we make our way into the church, I marvel at how

quickly Molly and Chad have become a part of my life. It seems like just yesterday that Molly started working at the farm, her skilled hands crafting beautiful wreaths that have become a hit with our customers. And Chad, with his boundless enthusiasm for everything from the tallest pines to the smallest pinecones, has brought a joy to the farm that I'd almost forgotten could exist there.

The service passes in a blur of hymns and prayers, but what stands out most is the feeling of Molly beside me, Chad's excited whispers as he tries to follow along, and the sense of peace that settles over me. For the first time in a long time, I'm not thinking about the pressures of the farm or the responsibilities weighing on my shoulders. Instead, I'm simply present, grateful for this moment and the people I'm sharing it with.

As we file out of the church after the service, I find myself reluctant to say goodbye. Before I can think better of it, I turn to Molly.

"I was thinking," I begin, suddenly feeling a bit nervous. "Would you and Chad like to come back to the farm for lunch? Nothing fancy, just some soup and sandwiches, but I thought it might be nice to spend some more time together."

Molly's face lights up, and I feel my heart skip a beat. "That sounds wonderful, Evan. We'd love to, wouldn't we, Chad?"

Chad nods enthusiastically. "Yeah! Can we make hot chocolate?"

I laugh, relief and joy mingling in my chest. "Sure thing, buddy."

EVAN

The drive back to the farm is filled with anticipation. I catch glimpses of Molly's car in my rearview mirror, and each time I do, I feel a surge of warmth. It's strange how something as simple as knowing they're following me home can make me feel so... complete.

As we pull up to the house, I see Chad's face press against the car window, his eyes wide with wonder. I have to admit, seeing the old cabin through their eyes makes me appreciate it anew.

The log cabin sits nestled among the evergreens, its weathered honey-brown timber a perfect complement to the surrounding forest. The wide front porch, with its wooden rocking chairs, looks inviting in the crisp winter air. I've spent many evenings there, watching the sun set over the distant mountains, but suddenly I can picture sharing those moments with Molly and Chad.

I park and hurry around to open Molly's door for her, earning a playful smile.

"Such a gentleman," she teases, her eyes sparkling with amusement.

I feel a blush creeping up my neck, but I can't help grinning back. "I try," I say with a wink.

Chad bursts out of the backseat, his energy seemingly boundless. "I'm hungry," he exclaims, already bounding up the porch steps.

As we follow at a more sedate pace, I find myself suddenly nervous. Molly's been to the farm many times now, working alongside me and bringing her own touch of warmth to the place. But inviting her into my home feels different. More intimate somehow.

I open the front door, stepping aside to let them enter first. The scent of the tall evergreen in the corner greets us, along with the lingering aroma of the coffee I'd made that morning.

"Oh, Evan," Molly breathes, taking in the cozy interior. "It's beautiful."

I watch as her eyes travel over the exposed wooden beams, the stone fireplace, the large windows that let in streams of winter sunlight. Chad is already exploring, peering at the family photos on the mantel and the antique farm tools that decorate the walls.

"Thanks," I say, feeling a mix of pride and self-consciousness. "It's home."

Molly turns to me, her expression soft and understanding. "It's perfect," she says firmly. "It feels just like you."

Her words pour through me like a hot liquid, warming me from the inside out. Because that's exactly what it is—this old cabin is a reflection of me, of my family's history, of the life I've built here. And having Molly and Chad here, seeing it through their eyes, makes me appreciate it in a whole new way.

"Come on," I say, clearing my throat against the sudden lump of emotion. "Let me show you around, then we can get started on lunch."

I lead them through the house, pointing out various features and sharing little stories along the way. Chad is fascinated by everything, from the old photographs to the view of the Christmas tree farm from the upstairs windows.

In the kitchen, Molly runs her hand along the smooth surface of the farmhouse table. "This is gorgeous," she says. "Did you make it?"

I nod, feeling a surge of pride. "My grandfather taught me woodworking when I was a kid. We made this table together the summer before he passed away."

Molly's eyes soften. "That's beautiful, Evan. What a wonderful way to remember him."

As we prepare lunch together, moving around the kitchen with an ease that surprises me, I imagine more days like this. More shared meals, more laughter echoing off these old wooden walls, more moments of quiet connection as we build something together—whether it's a simple soup, or a life intertwined.

Later, as we sit around the table enjoying our meal, I watch Molly and Chad. The way Molly's eyes crinkle at the corners when she laughs at Chad's jokes. The way Chad looks at me with a mix of admiration and curiosity that makes my heart swell. And I realize that this is what I've been missing all along.

It's not just about having people in the house, filling the empty spaces with noise and life. It's about sharing this part of myself—my home, my history, my heart—with people who understand its value. People who see the beauty in this life I've sometimes struggled to appreciate.

As the afternoon wears on, with Chad exploring the yard and Molly and I talking on the porch, I feel a sense of peace settle over me. It's not just the familiar comfort of my home, or the inspiring words from the morning's sermon. It's the realization that, for the first time in a long time, I'm exactly where I want to be.

As the sun dips toward the horizon, painting the sky in vibrant hues of orange and pink, I know our time together is coming to an end. But instead of the usual melancholy that comes with goodbyes, I feel a sense of anticipation.

Because I know this is just the beginning.

Fifteen

BETTY

Appearing on the outskirts of Evan Lawson's Christmas tree farm, I make my way towards the rustic barn that serves as the centerpiece of the property, and can't stop from smiling at the sight of families milling about, their laughter and excited chatter filling the air. Children dash between the rows of evergreens, playing hide and seek among the fragrant branches, while parents debate the merits of Douglas firs versus blue spruces. It's a scene of pure holiday joy, and my heart is full of Christmas spirit.

I spot Evan near the barn, his tall frame easy to pick out as he helps a young couple secure a tree to the roof of their car.

As I approach, I overhear the tail end of his conversation with the couple.

"...and remember, keep it watered. A thirsty tree is a fire hazard," Evan says, his deep voice carrying a note of genuine concern.

The young woman smiles up at him. "We will. Thank you so much for all your help. This is going to be the perfect Christmas tree for our first holiday as a married couple."

Evan's face features a warm smile. "I'm glad I could help. Merry Christmas to you both."

As the couple drives away, I make my way over to him. "That was a lovely thing you did," I say, my voice carrying the slight quaver I've learned to associate with my earthly form. "Helping that young couple start their Christmas traditions."

Evan turns to me, his blue eyes warming as he recognizes me. "Oh, hey Betty. Just doing my job, that's all."

I shake my head, allowing a knowing smile to play across my lips. "It's more than that, and you know it. You have a gift for making people feel welcome here, for helping them create memories. That's something special."

"Maybe so." He grins and I'm so happy to see how far he's come since Molly and Chad came into his life.

As we turn back towards the barn, I notice a shift in the air. The wind has picked up, carrying with it the distinct scent of impending snow. I close my eyes for a moment, tapping into my angelic senses, and I'm hit with a wave of foreboding. A storm is coming, fiercer than anything Benton Falls has seen in years.

I'm about to warn Evan when I hear a familiar voice call out across the farm. "Evan."

We both turn to see Molly making her way towards us, her chestnut hair whipping about her face in the strengthening wind. Even from a distance, I can see the worry lines creasing her forehead, and I feel a surge of protectiveness towards this woman who has unknowingly become so central to my mission.

Evan straightens beside me, his entire demeanor changing at the sight of Molly. It's like watching a flower turn towards the sun, and I have to stifle a smile at the obviousness of his feelings.

"Molly," he says as she reaches us, his voice warm with affection. "Is everything okay?"

She tucks a wayward strand of hair behind her ear, her hazel eyes flickering between Evan and me. "I just saw there's a big storm coming. I better get Chad home."

"Of course," Evan is already nodding as he pulls his phone from his pocket. "Yep, looks like a big one is headed our way. Let me send some extra firewood with you, just in case."

As Evan hurries off towards the woodpile, I turn to Molly with a gentle smile. "It will all be okay," I tell her.

Molly's shoulders relax slightly at my words. "I hope so. I just... I worry, you know?"

I reach out and squeeze her hand, channeling a bit of heavenly comfort through the touch. "That's what mothers do best."

She smiles, but her eyes are filled with uncertainty as Evan returns, his arms laden with firewood. "Here we go," he says, slightly out of breath. "This should keep you warm for a good long while."

As he loads the wood into the trunk of Molly's car, I notice the way their hands brush, the lingering glances they share. The love blooming between them is almost palpable, a warm glow that seems to push back against the gathering darkness of the approaching storm.

"Thank you, Evan," Molly says as he closes her trunk. "I don't know what we'd do without you."

Evan's cheeks redden slightly, and he shoves his hands in his pockets. "It's nothing, really. Just... just be safe, okay? This storm looks like it might be a bad one."

Molly nods, her eyes locking with his for a moment longer than necessary. "We will. You too, Evan. Take care of yourself."

As we watch Molly drive away, I can feel the shift in Evan's energy. The restlessness that had that once plagued him has been replaced by a fierce protectiveness. He may not realize it yet, but Molly and Chad have already become his world.

The wind howls around us, and I shiver, not entirely for show. "We should start battening down the hatches," I say, eyeing the darkening sky. "This storm isn't going to pull any punches."

Evan nods, his jaw set with determination. "You're right. Betty, you should go home before it starts."

"I'm an old farm girl at heart. I'm happy to stick around and help. Let's get everyone off the farm and make sure everything's secure."

"Are you sure?" Evan wants to talk me out of it. I'm sure he's thinking I'm more of a liability than anything else.

"I'm sure. Now let's go."

As we hurry to close up shop and ensure the safety of

the last few customers, I can't shake the feeling that this storm is more than just a weather event. It's an opportunity—a catalyst for change in Evan's life. And as his guardian angel in training, it's my job to make sure he weathers it in more ways than one.

The next few hours pass in a flurry of activity. Evan and I work side by side, securing loose items, checking on the animals in the barn, and making sure all the farm equipment is safely stored away. As the last customer drives off, the first fat snowflakes begin to fall, quickly blanketing the ground in white.

I watch as Evan stands on the porch of his log cabin, his eyes scanning the horizon with a mix of awe and concern. The wind whips around us, carrying with it the promise of a long, cold night ahead.

"I've never seen a storm move in this fast," he mutters, more to himself than to me. "Glad we sent Paul and Seth home when Molly and Chad left. I hope everyone made it home safely."

I can sense the worry radiating off him in waves, and I know exactly where his thoughts are headed. Sure enough, he turns to me, his blue eyes dark with concern. He pulls his phone from his pocket, glances at the screen, and shakes it in frustration.

"Betty, I hate to ask, but would you mind holding down the fort here for a bit? I just... I need to check on Molly and Chad. Make sure they're okay."

I nod, trying to hide my smile. This is exactly the kind of selfless action I've been hoping to see from Evan.

"Of course, dear. Don't you worry about a thing here. Go make sure they're safe."

He gives me a grateful smile before dashing inside to grab his keys. As I watch him drive off, his truck disappearing into the swirling snow, I close my eyes and focus my angelic senses. I can feel the storm's fury building, the raw power of nature unleashed. It's both terrifying and exhilarating.

I know I should stay put, play my role as the helpful volunteer, but something tugs at my heart. A whisper of divine intuition tells me that Evan might need more than just his own determination to make it safely to Molly's house.

Quickly, I pull the Miracle Card from my pocket and request invisibility, something only full guardian angels are allowed, as I transport myself to the cab of Evan's truck.

The journey is treacherous. The snow falls so thickly that it's almost impossible to see more than a few feet ahead. More than once, I have to use my angelic abilities to subtly guide Evan's truck away from hidden patches of ice or fallen branches.

As we near Molly's neighborhood, I can sense Evan's rising panic. The streets are nearly impassable; the snow piling up faster than the plows can clear it. But his determination never wavers. If anything, the challenging conditions seem to strengthen his resolve.

Finally, we turn onto Molly's street. Her house is dark, the power clearly out. Evan's truck skids to a stop in front of the driveway, and he's out the door before the engine has even fully quieted, plowing through knee-deep snow towards the front porch.

I appear on the sidewalk, just in time to see Molly throw open the door, a flashlight in her hand and relief written all over her face.

"Evan!" she calls out, her voice barely audible over the howling wind. "What are you doing here?"

He reaches the porch, covered in snow, but grinning like a man who's just won the lottery. "I had to make sure you and Chad were okay. The storm... it's worse than they predicted."

Molly's eyes shine with unshed tears as she ushers him inside. "You drove all the way out here in this? Evan, you could have been hurt!"

As the door closes behind them, shutting out the storm, I'm filled with joy. This is love, pure and simple. The kind of love that braves storms and defies logic. The kind of love that changes lives.

I close my eyes, sending up a silent prayer of thanks. My job isn't done yet—far from it. But in this moment, watching Evan choose to put Molly and Chad's safety above his own comfort, I know we're on the right track.

The storm rages on around me, but I barely feel the cold. Instead, I'm filled with a sense of purpose and hope. Because inside that darkened house, illuminated only by flashlights and the warm glow of a fireplace, something beautiful is happening. A family is coming together, finding strength and comfort in each other's presence.

And isn't that, after all, what Christmas is truly about?

I leave Evan and Molly to carry out my duties at the farm. As I return to the barn, I can sense the anxiety of the animals—the horses stamping nervously in their stalls, the barn cats huddled together in the hayloft, and their worried voices in my head. Using my angelic abilities, I send out waves of calming energy, soothing their fears. It's a small thing, perhaps, in the grand scheme of things, but it feels important. These creatures are under Evan's care, and by extension, under mine.

As I move through the barn, checking on each animal and securing any loose items that might pose a danger, I reflect on Evan's journey. When I first began watching over him, he was a man adrift, tied to this farm more out of duty than love. But in the weeks since Molly and Chad entered his life, I've seen a change in him. A softening, a rediscovery of joy in the simple things.

A strong gust of wind rattles the barn doors, and I hurry to secure them more tightly. As I do, I glimpse the farmhouse through the swirling snow. The windows are dark, the power clearly out here as well. Closing my eyes, I focus my energy on the farmhouse. I can't restore the power—that's beyond my abilities as a trainee—but I can create a bubble of warmth, a pocket of safety in the midst of the storm.

It's a subtle thing, something Evan might not even consciously notice, but it will be there when he returns, a silent comfort in the darkness.

As I complete this task, I feel a familiar presence

materialize beside me. I turn to see Henry, my mentor, his kind eyes twinkling with approval.

"Well done, Betty," he says, his voice carrying the warmth of a summer breeze even amid this winter storm. "You're learning to use your abilities with great discretion."

I feel a flush of pride at his words, followed quickly by a twinge of uncertainty. "I hope I'm not overstepping," I confess. "It's so tempting sometimes to just... fix everything for him."

Henry nods, his expression understanding. "That's the greatest challenge we face as guardians," he says. "Knowing when to act and when to step back. But you're finding the balance admirably."

He gestures towards the farmhouse, barely visible through the falling snow. "Your actions tonight—guiding Evan safely to Molly's house, calming the animals here, creating that pocket of warmth in the house—they're all perfect examples of how we can influence without interfering. You're giving Evan the tools he needs to grow to realize his own potential."

His words fill me with a warmth that rivals any earthly fire. "Thank you, Henry. I just hope it's enough. Evan's come so far, but he still struggles with fully embracing this life, this farm."

Henry's eyes twinkle with a knowing light. "Ah, but that's where tonight comes in. Sometimes, it takes a storm to help us appreciate the shelter we have."

I ponder his words, sensing the deeper meaning

behind them. "You think this blizzard will help Evan see the value of what he has here?"

"I think," Henry says carefully, "that being there for Molly and Chad in their time of need will show Evan a side of himself he's been hesitant to embrace. The protector, the provider, the man who finds joy in caring for others."

I nod, understanding dawning. "And in doing so, he might realize that the very things he's been yearning for—purpose, connection, love—have been here all along."

"Precisely," Henry beams at me. "You're catching on quickly, Betty. Now, let's see how our young friend is faring, shall we?"

With a wave of his hand, Henry creates a shimmering window in the air before us. Through it, we can see into Molly's living room. The scene that unfolds warms my heart more than any angelic power ever could.

Evan is kneeling before the fireplace, carefully building up a fire. The warm glow illuminates his face, highlighting the concentration in his eyes and the gentle set of his mouth. Molly sits nearby, wrapped in a blanket, watching him with a mixture of gratitude and something deeper, something she might not even recognize yet as love.

Chad bounces into view, his arms full of board games. "Can we play Monopoly, Mom? Please?" His excited voice carries through the ethereal window, bringing a smile to my face.

Molly laughs, the sound like music in the storm-muffled room. "I don't know, honey. It's getting pretty late..."

"Aw, come on," Evan chimes in, turning from the now-crackling fire with a boyish grin. "What's a power outage for if not staying up late and playing board games?"

The joy on Chad's face at Evan's support is palpable, and I watch as Molly's resolve melts away. "Alright, alright," she concedes with a mock sigh. "But just one game."

As they set up the board, I watch the easy way they move around each other, the casual touches, the shared smiles. They look, for all the world, like a family. And judging by the contentment radiating from Evan, I think he's starting to see it, too.

"You see?" Henry's voice breaks into my reverie. "This is what Evan needed. Not a grand adventure or a life-changing revelation, but this: a quiet evening, a chance to be there for the people he cares about, to see himself as an essential part of their lives."

I nod, unable to tear my eyes away from the scene. "It's beautiful," I murmur. "I've never seen him so... at peace."

Henry lays a gentle hand on my shoulder. "That, my dear, is the magic of love and gratitude. When we open our hearts to others, when we learn to appreciate the blessings we have, we find a contentment that no worldly adventure could ever provide."

As we watch, Evan rolls the dice, moving his piece around the board. He lands on one of Molly's properties, and she gleefully demands payment, her eyes sparkling with mischief. Evan groans dramatically, handing over the colorful money with an exaggerated pout that sends Chad into fits of giggles.

It's such a simple moment, but it's filled with more joy, more genuine connection, than I've seen from Evan in all the weeks I've been watching over him. In this candlelit room, with the storm raging outside, he's found a peace that had eluded him on even the calmest days.

"You've done well, Betty," Henry says. "Your guidance, your subtle nudges, they've helped lead Evan to this moment. But remember, the journey isn't over. There will be more moments when Evan will need to choose gratitude over restlessness, love over fear."

I nod, feeling the weight of responsibility settle on my shoulders once more. But it's a welcome weight, a reminder of the important work we do. "I'm ready," I tell Henry, my voice filled with determination. "Whatever comes next, I'll be there to guide him."

Henry smiles, his form already fading as he prepares to return to the celestial realm. "I know you will, Betty. You're going to make an excellent guardian angel."

As Henry disappears, I turn my attention back to the shimmering window. The Monopoly game is in full swing now, with Chad gleefully building houses on his properties and Molly and Evan engaged in some good-natured haggling over a trade.

I watch as Evan leans back, surveying the scene before him. There's a softness in his eyes, a quiet wonder, as if he's seeing everything - the room, the game, Molly and

Chad - in a new light. In that moment, I can almost hear his thoughts, can feel the realization dawning in his heart: This is what he's been searching for—this sense of belonging, of being needed and wanted, of having a place in the world that's uniquely his.

The storm continues to rage outside, but within the warm circle of firelight, a different kind of magic is at work. It's the magic of family, of love freely given and gratefully received. And as I watch, I know that this night will be a turning point for Evan. A night when the blessings he's always had finally come into focus, shining brighter than any far-off dream ever could.

I allow the window to fade, the image of the happy trio lingering in my mind. There's more work to be done, more guidance to be given, but for now, I'm content to celebrate the moment.

Sixteen

EVAN

Snowflakes fall in a slow flurry as I step out of my truck, the gravel under the snow crunching beneath my boots. The sun, a pale disk in the winter sky, casts long shadows across the town park. I take a deep breath, inhaling the scent of pine and cinnamon that seems to permeate everything in Benton Falls during the holiday season.

As I adjust my scarf, smoothing down the soft wool, I catch sight of Molly's car pulling into the parking lot. My heart does a little Christmas Polka dance as she parks and helps Chad out of the backseat.

Chad spots me first, his face lighting up with that infectious grin of his. "Evan." he calls out, waving enthusiastically. "Over here."

I wave as I smile. "Hey there."

As they make their way over, I can't help but grin like a kid on Christmas morning.

"Good evening," Molly says as they reach me, her eyes

warm with affection. "I hope we didn't keep you waiting."

"Not at all," I assure her, resisting the urge to reach out and tuck a stray strand of hair behind her ear. "I just got here myself."

Chad, bouncing on his toes with barely contained energy, looks up at me with wide eyes. "Is the ice rink ready, Evan? Can we go skating now?"

I chuckle, ruffling his sandy hair. "It sure is, buddy. But let's make sure your mom is ready first, okay?"

Molly gives me a grateful smile. "I'm as ready as I'll ever be. It's been years since I've been on skates, though. I might need someone to hold on to."

Her words send a warmth spreading through my chest, and I stand a little straighter. "Well, you're in luck," I tell her. "I happen to be an excellent skating partner."

As we make our way towards the rink, I can't resist thinking about how effortlessly Molly and Chad have become a part of my life. It feels like it was always meant to be this way. Like we were meant to be working at the farm together, her skilled hands crafting beautiful wreaths and making everything perfect for the townspeople. I feel drawn towards Molly and Chad and their happiness and their joy. I feel like we belong together in Benton Falls.

Each December, the town park is transformed for the Christmas Market, a winter wonderland of booths and holiday magic. Twinkling lights are strung between the trees, casting a warm glow over the fresh snow. There are people eating, shopping, and just enjoying the season. Of course, the ice rink gleaming in the center of the park, a temporary addition for the holiday season, is one of the market's main attractions.

"Wow," Molly breathes beside me, her eyes wide with wonder. "It's like something out of a Hallmark movie."

I nod, feeling a swell of pride in my hometown. "Benton Falls knows how to do Christmas right. Year after year, it's still something to behold."

We make our way to the skate rental booth, where Noah Montgomery greets us with a knowing smile. "Evening, Evan," he says, his eyes twinkling as he glances between me and Molly. "And who might these fine folks be?"

"This is Molly and her son, Chad," I introduce them, feeling a warmth spread through me at being able to do so. "They're... friends of mine."

The word 'friends' feels inadequate, but I'm not sure what else to call them. We haven't put a label on whatever this is growing between us, and I don't want to presume. Still, the way Noah's smile widens tells me he sees right through me.

"Well, any friends of Evan's are friends of mine," he says warmly. "What sizes can I get for you folks?"

As we lace up our skates, I watch Molly's hands tremble slightly. She wasn't kidding about being out of practice. I reach out, covering her hand with mine. "Hey," I say softly. "You okay?"

She looks up at me, a mix of excitement and nervousness in her eyes. "Just a little scared," she admits. "It's been so long, and I was never very good to begin with."

I squeeze her hand gently. "Don't worry. I've got you. We'll take it nice and slow, okay?"

The gratitude in her smile makes my heart skip a beat. "Okay," she nods. "I trust you."

Those three words, so simple and yet so profound, settle into my chest like a warm ember. I've spent so long feeling restless, yearning for something more, something different. But in this moment, with Molly's hand in mine and Chad's excited chatter filling the air, I realize that everything I've been searching for is right here in Benton Falls.

We make our way to the rink, Chad practically vibrating with excitement. He's clearly more confident on skates than his mom, probably thanks to hours spent at the local roller rink. As soon as his blades touch the ice, he's off, wobbling slightly but picking up speed with each stride.

"Be careful, honey!" Molly calls after him, her grip on my arm tightening.

I chuckle, placing my hand over hers reassuringly. "He'll be fine. Kids are like rubber at that age. Besides, look how much fun he's having."

And it's true. Chad's face is alight with joy as he makes his way around the rink, waving to us each time he passes. His enthusiasm is infectious, drawing smiles from everyone he passes.

"Ready?" I ask Molly, gently guiding her towards the ice.

She takes a deep breath, nodding. "As I'll ever be."

We step onto the ice together, and I feel Molly tense

beside me as her skates slide slightly. I tighten my grip on her arm, steadying her. "I've got you," I murmur. "Just take it slow. Small steps."

Gradually, we begin to move, gliding across the ice in small, careful strokes. Molly's grip on my arm is tight, but with each passing minute, I can feel her relaxing, growing more confident.

"That's it," I encourage her. "You're doing great."

She looks up at me, a mixture of pride and amusement in her eyes. "I feel like a newborn fawn," she laughs. "All wobbly legs and uncertainty."

I grin, enjoying the sound of her laughter. "Well, you're the most graceful newborn fawn I've ever seen."

As we make our way around the rink, I'm acutely aware of every point of contact between us. The warmth of her body pressed against my side, the way her hand fits perfectly in mine, the sweet scent of her shampoo carried on the winter breeze. It's intoxicating in the best possible way.

We pass by one of the warming stations, where families are huddled together, sipping hot beverages and watching the skaters. The air is filled with the sound of laughter and Christmas carols playing softly from speakers hidden in the trees.

"You know," I say, as we complete another circuit of the rink, "after we're done here, we should check out some booths. And I hear there's a reindeer petting zoo this year."

Molly's eyes light up at the suggestion. "That sounds wonderful. Chad would love the reindeer."

As if on cue, Chad zooms past us, now part of a small pack of kids playing some kind of tag game on skates. "Mom! Evan! Did you see how fast I was going?" he shouts, his voice filled with excitement.

"We see you, honey!" Molly calls back. "You're doing great!"

As we watch Chad zip around the rink, I'm struck by how much he's grown in the short time I've known him. Not just physically, but in confidence and spirit.

"He's really something, isn't he?" I say.

Molly nods, her eyes following her son's progress around the rink. "He is. You know, when his dad left, I was so worried. About everything. Whether we'd fit in, whether I'd be able to provide for him, whether he'd be happy... But now..."

She trails off, and I give her hand a gentle squeeze, encouraging her to continue.

"Now," she says, her voice filled with wonder, "I'm not so worried anymore. This town, the farm, you..." She looks up at me, her eyes shining. "It's like we've found where we belong."

My heart swells at her words, a lump forming in my throat. Because I feel it too. This sense of rightness, of coming home. For so long, I've felt tied to Benton Falls by duty and obligation. But now, with Molly and Chad in my life, I'm seeing it all through new eyes.

The twinkling lights aren't just decorations, they're beacons of warmth and community. The familiar faces around us aren't just neighbors, they're friends, family.

And the farm, which for so long felt like a burden, now feels like the foundation for something beautiful.

"I'm glad to hear you feel that way too," I tell her, my voice rough with emotion. "Because I can't imagine this place without you two in it."

For a moment, we just look at each other, the rest of the world fading away. I'm lost in the warmth of Molly's eyes, the soft curve of her smile. The urge to kiss her is almost overwhelming, but I hold back, knowing Chad is in the vicinity.

"Mom, Evan," Chad calls, right on cue. "Can we go see the reindeer now? Please?"

We both laugh, the spell broken but not forgotten. "Sure thing, buddy," I call back. "Let's get our skates off and we'll go look."

As we make our way off the ice, I keep a steady hand on Molly's back, guiding her. She's more confident now, but the transition from ice to solid ground can be tricky. Once we're safely off the ice, we remove our skates and return them to Noah.

"You folks have a wonderful evening now," he says with a wink. "Enjoy the market!"

As we walk among the booths, each one decorated with twinkling lights and garlands. The air is filled with the scent of mulled cider and cloves, mingled with the savory aroma of roasting chestnuts. Chad's eyes grow wide with wonder. "Wow," he breathes. "It's like the North Pole!"

Molly and I exchange a smile over his head. "It sure is,

buddy," I say. "Now, what should we check out first? The reindeer or the hot chocolate?"

As Chad debates this crucial decision, I catch Molly's eye. The joy and contentment I see reflected there mirror my own feelings perfectly. In this moment, surrounded by the magic of Christmas in Benton Falls, I know that I'm exactly where I'm meant to be.

Seventeen

EVAN

The scent of gingerbread and sugar wafts through the air as I push open the heavy wooden doors of the Benton Falls Community Center. The warmth inside is a stark contrast to the brisk December evening, and I feel my cheeks tingle as they adjust to the change in temperature. Beside me, Chad lets out an excited whoop, his eyes wide with wonder as he takes in the festive scene before us.

"Wow!" he exclaims, tugging on Molly's hand. "Mom, look at all the gingerbread houses. They're even better than the ones we saw at the start of the contest!"

Molly laughs, her hazel eyes twinkling in the soft glow of the twinkling lights strung across the ceiling. "You're right, honey. The professional entries are really something else, aren't they?"

I'm smiling at their interaction as happiness permeates all around me. It's moments like these—simple, joyful, full of wonder - that have become increasingly precious to me over the past few weeks.

As we make our way further into the hall, I'm struck by the sheer artistry on display. The gingerbread structures before us are true masterpieces, ranging from intricate castles dusted with powdered sugar snow to elaborate recreations of famous landmarks. The air is filled with the excited chatter of families and friends admiring the edible works of art, punctuated by the soft strains of Christmas carols playing in the background.

"I can't believe how detailed some of these are," Molly murmurs, leaning in close to examine a miniature version of the Eiffel Tower. Her shoulder brushes against mine, and I feel a jolt of electricity at the contact. "Look at the tiny elevator inside. You can almost see it moving!"

I nod, equally impressed. "The level of skill here is incredible. It's hard to believe these are edible."

Chad, who has been darting from display to display, suddenly calls out, "Evan! Come look at this one! It looks just like your farm!"

Curious, Molly and I follow Chad to a gingerbread creation near the back of the hall. As we approach, I feel my breath catch in my throat. There, rendered in painstaking detail, is a perfect miniature of Lawson Christmas Tree Farm.

The gingerbread barn is an exact replica of the one my great-grandfather built, right down to the weathervane on top. Rows of tiny sugar cone trees stretch out from the barn, their green frosting needles dusted with a light coating of coconut "snow". There's even a tiny gingerbread figure in a red flannel shirt standing among the trees, a minuscule axe in hand.

"Is that... supposed to be me?" I ask, leaning in for a closer look.

Molly giggles, a sound that never fails to make my heart skip a beat. "I think it is! Look, they even got your perpetual five o'clock shadow."

I run a hand over my stubbled jaw, feeling a mix of embarrassment and pride. "I didn't realize I was such a recognizable figure in town."

"Are you kidding?" a familiar voice chimes in from behind us. We turn to see Betty approaching, a steaming cup of hot cocoa in her hands. "Evan, dear, you're practically a Benton Falls institution. The farm has been part of this community for generations."

There's a twinkle in Betty's eye as she says this, and I'm struck once again by how much she reminds me of my grandmother. She has the same wise, knowing look, as if she can see right through to the heart of things.

"It's a beautiful piece," Molly says, gesturing to the gingerbread farm. "Do you know who made it?"

Betty nods, a proud smile spreading across her face. "That would be Chef Antoine from the Grand Hotel in the city. He's been fascinated by our little town ever since he visited for the fall festival. Talented man, isn't he?"

As we continue to admire Chef Antoine's handiwork, I find myself lost in thought. The gingerbread version of the farm looks so idyllic, so perfect. Is that how others see it? How they see me? The steadfast farmer, rooted to the land, a pillar of the community?

EVAN

I glance at Molly, watching as she points out details of the gingerbread farm to Chad. Her face is animated, her eyes bright with excitement. Chad hangs on her every word, his own face a mirror of her joy. The sight of them together, so happy, so at home here in Benton Falls, fills me with a warmth I can't quite name.

"It's something special, isn't it?" Betty's voice breaks into my reverie, and I turn to find her watching me with a knowing smile.

"The gingerbread house?" I ask, though I have a feeling she's talking about something else entirely.

Betty shakes her head, her eyes twinkling. "Family, Evan. The way you three fit together. It's a beautiful thing to see."

I feel a blush creeping up my neck at her words. "We're not... I mean, Molly and I aren't..."

"Oh, I know," Betty says, patting my arm gently. "But sometimes the best families are the ones we choose for ourselves. And sometimes, the things we've been searching for have been right in front of us all along."

Before I can respond, Chad's excited voice cuts through the air. "Mom! Evan! Can we go see the judging? I want to see which one wins!"

Molly laughs, ruffling Chad's hair affectionately. "Of course, honey. Let's go find a good spot to watch from."

As they move away, Betty gives me one last meaningful look. "Don't let fear of change keep you from embracing what's right in front of you, Evan. Sometimes, the biggest adventures are the ones we never expected to have."

With that cryptic advice, she vanishes into the crowd, leaving me to ponder her words. I shake my head, marveling at Betty's ability to see right to the heart of things. She's right, of course. The thought of fully embracing this new dynamic with Molly and Chad is both thrilling and terrifying. But as I watch them make their way through the crowded hall, Chad's excitement infectious and Molly's laughter ringing out above the general hubbub, I can't deny the pull I feel towards them.

I'm about to follow when I hear a voice call my name.

"Evan. There you are. I was hoping I'd run into you again."

I turn to see Morgan Caldwell approaching, her camera crew in tow. She looks as polished and professional as she did at the tree lighting ceremony last week, her dark hair styled in sleek waves, her outfit screaming big city success.

"Morgan," I greet her, trying to keep my voice neutral. Our last encounter left me feeling unsettled. "How's the coverage going?"

She beams clearly in her element. "It's going great! The response to our segment on the tree lighting has been fantastic. People love the small-town Christmas charm of Benton Falls."

I nod, a mix of pride and unease swirling in my chest. It's gratifying to know that others appreciate the beauty of our town. "Listen, Evan," Morgan continues, her voice dropping to a more intimate tone. "I got an idea after I saw you a few weeks ago, presented it to my boss and he loved it. How would you feel about possibly appearing on the show?"

"Seriously?" I ask as a knot forms in my stomach. *Me on television?*

"Seriously," she smiles.

"I'm not sure I'm cut out for TV, Morgan."

She waves off my concerns. "Nonsense. You'd be perfect. Handsome, rugged tree farmer keeping Christmas traditions alive? The audience would eat it up." She pauses, her eyes glinting with excitement. "And what if we did a series of segments? Not just on the farm, but on Christmas traditions around the world? You could travel with us, Evan. See all those places you used to dream about."

Her words hit me like a punch to the gut. Travel. Adventure. All the things I once dreamed of, suddenly within reach. It's tempting, so tempting.

But then I glance across the room, my eyes finding Molly and Chad. They're standing near the judges' table, Chad on his tiptoes trying to get a better view, Molly's hand resting protectively on his shoulder. And I feel a different kind of pull, one that has nothing to do with faraway places and everything to do with the life I've been building here.

"I... I don't know, Morgan," I say, my voice hesitant. "It's a lot to think about."

She nods, understanding in her eyes. "Of course. It's a big decision. Why don't you take my card? Think it over, talk to your... friends. Call me if you're interested, or if you have questions."

I take the card, turning it over in my hands. It feels weighty, laden with possibility. "Thanks, Morgan. I will."

As she moves away to rejoin her crew, I stand there for a moment, my mind whirling. The opportunity Morgan's offering is everything I once thought I wanted. A chance to see the world, to break free from the responsibilities that have tied me to Benton Falls for so long.

But as I make my way over to Molly and Chad, watching as their faces light up at my approach, I remember how blessed my life is now because they're a part of it and I'm not sure how to feel about Morgan's offer.

"Everything okay?" Molly asks as I reach them, her brow furrowing slightly in concern. "You look like you've got a lot on your mind."

I shake my head, forcing a smile. "Just... thinking about some things. Nothing to worry about."

Chad tugs on my sleeve, oblivious to the undercurrent of tension. "Evan, they're about to announce the winners. Do you think the farm one will win?"

I ruffle his hair, grateful for the distraction. "I don't know, buddy. There are a lot of amazing entries here. But I think it's got a good shot."

As the head judge steps up to the microphone, I feel Molly's hand slip into mine. It's a small gesture, probably unconscious on her part, but it grounds me. In that moment, with Chad's excited whispers and Molly's warm presence beside me, I know that no matter what opportunities might come my way, my heart belongs right here in Benton Falls.

EVAN

The judge clears his throat, and the hall falls silent. "Ladies and gentlemen, after careful consideration, we are ready to announce the winners of this year's Professional Gingerbread House Contest."

As he lists the runners-up, I find my mind drifting. The gingerbread houses around us are incredible, true works of art. But they're also temporary, destined to crumble and fade. What I'm building with Molly and Chad, though... that has the potential to last. To grow into something beautiful and enduring.

"And the grand prize winner is..." the judge pauses for dramatic effect, "Chef Antoine, for his charming and detailed recreation of the Lawson Christmas Tree Farm!"

The hall erupts in applause. Chad jumps up and down, his excitement palpable. "Evan! Your farm won! Your farm won!"

I laugh, caught up in his enthusiasm. "Well, Chef Antoine's version of it did, anyway."

Molly squeezes my hand, her eyes shining. "It's because the real thing is so special," she says. "He just captured what we all see when we look at your farm."

Her words should warm me, but instead, I feel a knot forming in my stomach. As we make our way towards the winning display, where Chef Antoine is standing next to his artwork with a beaming smile, I can't shake the feeling of unease that's settled over me.

The gingerbread farm glitters under the lights, a perfect miniature of the place I've called home all my life. But as I stare at it, I'm struck by how small it seems. How confined. Is this how others see my world? A quaint, picturesque setting, but ultimately limited?

I realize it's just a replica, a sweet but fleeting representation. The real farm, with all its challenges and rewards, is waiting for me. And so are Molly and Chad, their presence in my life more nourishing than any confectionary creation could ever be. So why can't I quit thinking about Morgan's offer?

As the evening winds down and we prepare to leave, Morgan catches my eye from across the room. She raises an eyebrow, a silent question about her offer. I feel a surge of longing that takes me by surprise. The idea of travel, of new experiences, of breaking free from the familiar... it tugs at me with more pull than I'd like to admit. But I also feel a yearning towards Molly and Chad. A tug that is strong and pure. Like they might be just the thing that makes me whole. I give Morgan a small smile and a shrug of my shoulders. There will be time for a proper response later, when I have it figured out.

"Evan? Are you ready to go?" Molly's voice breaks into my thoughts. She's helping Chad into his coat, her face flushed with happiness from the evening's excitement.

"Yeah, just... just give me a moment," I say, my voice sounding distant even to my own ears.

I watch as Molly leads Chad towards the exit, their heads bent together as they chat about their favorite gingerbread houses. They look so at home here, so content. And yet, I can't shake the feeling that I'm standing at a crossroads.

EVAN

On one side is the life I've always known - the farm, the responsibilities, the familiar rhythms of Benton Falls. It's a good life, filled with warmth and community. Molly and Chad are part of that now, bringing a joy I never expected to find.

But on the other side is the unknown - the chance to see the world, to push myself in ways I never have before. Morgan's offer dangles before me like a shiny ornament, tempting and bright.

I finger the business card in my pocket, the edges already curling from how many times I've taken it out to look at it. The decision I face seems to loom larger with each passing moment.

As I finally make my way to join Molly and Chad, my steps feel heavy. The contentment I felt earlier has been replaced by a restlessness I thought I'd left behind. The warmth of the community center gives way to the chilly night air, and I shiver, but not from the cold.

"Are you sure you're okay?" Molly asks as I approach, her brow furrowing slightly in concern.

I force a smile, but it feels brittle on my face. "Yeah, fine..."

Chad, oblivious to the tension, chatters happily about wanting to make a gingerbread house of his own. Molly laughs at his enthusiasm, but I catch her glancing at me with worried eyes.

As we walk to our cars, the festive lights of Benton Falls twinkling around us, I'm acutely aware of the weight of the decision before me. The life I've been building here, with its unexpected joys and deepening connections, suddenly feels both precious and precarious.

I help Chad into Molly's car, then turn to say goodnight. Molly's eyes search my face, and I know she can sense my unease.

"Evan," she starts, her voice soft with concern, "if there's anything you want to talk about..."

I shake my head, not trusting myself to speak. Instead, I lean in and place a gentle kiss on her cheek. "Goodnight, Molly. I'll see you tomorrow at the farm."

As I walk to my truck, I can feel her gaze on my back, while the card in my pocket seems to burn, a reminder of the choice I have to make. I climb into the cab of my truck, the familiar scent of pine and leather doing little to calm my churning emotions. As I drive home through the quiet streets of Benton Falls, my thoughts continue to war one with another.

The farm looms ahead, dark and silent under the starry sky. I park and sit for a long moment, engine off, staring at the house that's been in my family for generations. I pull out Morgan's card one last time, staring at the embossed letters until they blur before my eyes. The promise of adventure, of a life beyond these familiar boundaries, calls to me with a siren song I thought I'd stopped hearing.

But then I think of Molly's warm smile, of Chad's infectious laughter, of the life I've been slowly building here. It's a good life, a meaningful one. Isn't it?

Later that night, as I get ready for bed, my mind continues to whirl. The gingerbread contest, meant to be a simple evening of festive fun, has instead cracked open a door I thought I'd firmly closed.

I lie awake long into the night, Morgan's offer and Molly's concerned face battling for dominance in my thoughts. The future, which had seemed so clear just hours ago, now stretches before me like an uncharted path, full of possibility and peril in equal measure.

Sleep, when it finally comes, is fitful and filled with dreams of faraway places and roads not taken.

And through it all, one question echoes: What do I really want?

Eighteen

BETTY

The air in the celestial realm shimmers with a soft, golden light as I walk through the halls of the Angel Institute. The familiar warmth of heaven envelops me, a stark contrast to the nippy winter air I've grown accustomed to in Benton Falls. Despite the comfort of this ethereal space, I feel a knot of anxiety forming in my celestial core.

"Betty," Henry's gentle voice breaks through my thoughts. "You look concerned. What troubles you, my dear?"

I turn to see my mentor coming towards me, his kind eyes twinkling with understanding. Even in this radiant realm, Henry's presence stands out, a beacon of wisdom and compassion.

"Oh, Henry," I sigh, the weight of my worries manifesting in a very human gesture. "It's Evan. He's at a crossroads, and I'm afraid he might make the wrong choice."

Henry nods, a knowing smile playing at the corners of his mouth. "Ah, yes. Morgan's job offer. It's quite the temptation, isn't it?"

I nod, feeling a surge of frustration. "It's everything he once thought he wanted - travel, adventure, freedom from the responsibilities of the farm. But he's come so far, Henry. He's found something beautiful with Molly and Chad. How can he even consider leaving that behind?"

Henry places a comforting hand on my shoulder, and I feel a wave of calm wash over me. "Remember, Betty, our role is not to make choices for our charges, but to guide them towards making the best choices for themselves."

"I know," I say, my voice tinged with a hint of earthly exasperation. "But it's so hard to watch him struggle when the answer seems so clear to me."

Henry chuckles, a sound like distant bells. "Clear to you, perhaps. But Evan must come to his own conclusions. That's the beauty and the challenge of free will."

I nod, knowing he's right, but still feeling the weight of my concern. "I just wish I could do more. Show him somehow what he'd be giving up if he left."

Henry's eyes twinkle with mischief. "Well, now that you mention it, I might have an idea. How would you like to try your hand at dream weaving?"

My celestial form practically vibrates with excitement. "Really? You think I'm ready for that?"

Henry nods, his expression turning serious. "I do. But remember, Betty, dreams are a delicate thing. We can offer guidance and show possibilities, but we cannot make the choice for Evan. The final decision must be his and his alone."

I nod solemnly, understanding the gravity of this new responsibility. "I understand, Henry. I'll be careful."

"I know you will," he says, his faith in me clear in his warm smile. "Now, let's get you prepared for this new adventure."

For the next few celestial moments (time works differently here in heaven), Henry guides me through the intricacies of dream weaving. It's a complex art, requiring a delicate balance of influence and restraint. We can't control dreams entirely—that would infringe on agency—but we can plant seeds, offer gentle nudges, create an environment conducive to revelation and growth.

As our lesson ends, I feel both exhilarated and humbled by this new ability. Henry places a hand on my shoulder, his touch infusing me with confidence and purpose.

"Remember, Betty," he says, his voice filled with warmth and wisdom, "your greatest tools are not these celestial abilities, impressive though they may be. Your greatest tools are love, compassion, and faith. Trust in those, and you can't go wrong."

I nod, feeling a swell of gratitude for this gentle mentor who has guided me so patiently. "Thank you, Henry. For everything."

With a final smile and a wave of his hand, Henry sends me back to Earth. I materialize on the outskirts of Evan's farm, the cold night air a shock to my senses after the warmth of the celestial realm. The farm is quiet, peaceful under its blanket of snow. In the distance, I can see a single light burning in the farmhouse window.

As I make my way towards the house, my mind is already working, planning how best to use my new ability to help Evan. Perhaps a dream of the farm in full summer bloom, to reinforce his growing appreciation for this place? Or a vision of a future Christmas, with Molly and Chad by his side, to nurture the seeds of love and family that are already taking root?

The possibilities are endless, and for a moment, I feel almost overwhelmed by the responsibility. But then I remember Henry's words. Love, compassion, faith. With those as my guide, I know I can't go wrong.

I pause at the edge of the porch, looking up at the star-filled sky. The beauty of it takes my breath away - a beauty I might once have taken for granted, but which now fills me with awe and gratitude. In this moment, I understand exactly what Evan is learning: that the most precious gifts are often the ones right in front of us, if only we have the wisdom to see them.

With a silent prayer, I enter the farmhouse, my celestial form passing through the walls as easily as if they were mist. Inside, the air is warm and fragrant with the scent of spice and evergreen. Chad's picture of the three of them on the tree farm hangs from the refrigerator. The sight brings a smile to my face.

As I continue to craft the dream, I feel Evan's breathing slow and deepen. He's drifting off, my celestial influence gently guiding him towards sleep. I watch as he exhales, Morgan's card slipping from his fingers to flutter to the floor.

With Evan now asleep, I can fully immerse myself in the dreamscape I'm creating. I pour all my love for this place, all my hope for Evan's future, into every detail. The dream expands, showing not just one perfect summer day, but a montage of moments:

Evan and Molly dancing under strings of fairy lights at a summer festival in town.

Chad's first day of school, with Evan and Molly walking him to the bus stop together.

A quiet evening by the fireplace, the three of them reading books and sipping hot cocoa.

Evan teaching Chad how to build a birdhouse, their laughter mingling with the sound of hammering.

Molly surprising Evan with a homemade birthday cake, her eyes shining with love.

Through it all, I weave a sense of contentment, of belonging, of a life rich with love and purpose. I show Evan the beauty of the life he's building here, the depth of the connections he's forming, the joy that comes from being truly rooted in a place and a community.

As the dream reaches its crescendo, I add one final scene: Evan, Molly, and Chad decorating the Christmas tree in the farmhouse. The room is warm and cozy, filled with the scent of pine and the sound of carols playing in the background. Chad places the star on top of the tree, perched on Evan's shoulders, while Molly looks on, her face glowing with happiness. As Chad comes down, they all embrace, a perfect family moment captured in the twinkling lights of the tree.

I step back, both literally and figuratively, from the dream I've woven. It's beautiful, filled with love and possibility. But as I watch Evan's sleeping form, I'm struck by a sudden doubt. Have I gone too far? Shown too much of what I want for him, rather than what he truly needs to see?

I shake off the doubt, reminding myself of Henry's teachings. This dream is just a suggestion, a glimpse of possibility.

The choice remains Evan's alone.

As the night wears on, I keep vigil over Evan's sleep, gently guiding his dreams when they veer towards anxiety or doubt. It's delicate work, requiring constant attention and adjustment. But as I watch the tension gradually ease from Evan's face, replaced by a small, contented smile, I feel a sense of accomplishment.

Just before dawn, I sense a shift in Evan's consciousness. He's starting to wake up. I quickly withdraw my influence, allowing his mind to transition naturally from the dream world to waking reality.

Evan stirs, lifting his head from the pillow with a soft groan. He blinks, looking around the room with a slightly dazed expression. He sits up and stretches before his eyes fall on Morgan's business card, lying forgotten on the floor, and I hold my breath (metaphorically speaking, of course) as I wait to see his reaction.

To my surprise and delight, Evan leans over, picks up the card and, after a moment's hesitation, tucks it away in the nightstand drawer instead of staring at it. It's a small gesture, but it fills me with hope.

As Evan heads to the bathroom to start his day, I allow myself a moment of quiet celebration. The dream seems to have had some effect, but I know the battle is far from over. Evan still has a difficult decision ahead of him.

After he showers and dresses, I watch as he moves through the farmhouse, pausing to straighten a photo of himself with Molly and Chad. His fingers linger on the frame, a soft smile playing at the corners of his mouth. When he steps outside, he takes a deep breath, inhaling the fresh winter air with what seems like newfound appreciation.

"It really is beautiful," he murmurs to himself, and I feel a surge of joy at his words.

But as I prepare to return to the celestial realm, doubt creeps in.

Have I done enough?

Will this one dream be sufficient to counter the allure of Morgan's offer?

The weight of Evan's decision hangs heavy in the air, and I wonder: in the battle between roots and wings, which will ultimately win out in Evan's heart?

Nineteen

EVAN

The scent of hot cider and pine fills the air as I adjust the collar of my wool coat, trying to ward off the cool December chill. Main Street is alive with the buzz of excitement, families and friends lining the sidewalks in anticipation of the annual Benton Falls Community Christmas Parade. Twinkling lights adorn every lamppost and storefront, transforming our little town into a winter wonderland.

I scan the crowd, searching for Molly and Chad. My heart skips a beat when I spot them near Violet's Diner, Molly's chestnut hair peeking out from beneath a jaunty red beret. Chad bounces beside her, his enthusiasm palpable even from a distance.

As I make my way towards them, weaving through the throng of excited townsfolk, I can't help but recall the amazing dreams I had last night, one right after another, images of me, Molly, and Chad as a family—I'm not sure what the dreams meant. Maybe I'd been visited by the Ghost of Christmas, but does that make me a Scrooge? I grin, shaking off the notion. I can't think about that now.

"Evan!" Chad's excited voice carries over the crowd. He waves frantically, nearly knocking off his own hat. "We saved you a spot!"

I grin as I reach them. "Thanks, buddy. Wouldn't want to miss the best view in town, would I?"

Molly's eyes meet mine, and the warmth in her gaze makes my heart flutter. "We were starting to think you might not make it," she says, her tone gently teasing.

"And miss seeing Santa? Not a chance," I reply, winking at Chad. The boy's eyes widen with excitement at the mention of Saint Nick.

As I settle in beside them, I'm acutely aware of Molly's presence. The soft scent of her perfume - something floral and delicate - mingles with the holiday aromas around us. Her shoulder brushes against mine as she shifts to make room, and even through layers of winter clothing, I feel a jolt of electricity at the contact.

"So, what's the inside scoop?" I ask, leaning in conspiratorially. "Any intel on this year's parade highlights?"

Chad pipes up immediately, his words tumbling out in a rush of excitement. "Maggie said the bakery made a giant gingerbread house float! And the hardware store is doing a workshop with moving elves. Oh, and the high school band has new uniforms that light up!"

I chuckle at his enthusiasm. "Sounds like it's going to be quite the spectacle. Can't wait to see it."

Molly smiles, her eyes twinkling in the glow of the streetlights. "Me too. And the parade will be even better now that you're here." She takes my hand. "Right where you belong."

Her words fill my heart with beats of joy and an unexpected pang of guilt. This is where I belong, with this community. So why am I still holding onto Morgan's business card? Why can't I shake the lingering doubt, the whisper of 'what if' that plagues me in quiet moments?

Before I can dwell on these thoughts, the sound of distant music catches our attention. Chad lets out an excited whoop. "It's starting!"

The parade kicks off with the Benton Falls High School marching band, their newly illuminated uniforms living up to the hype. They play a rousing rendition of "Jingle Bells" that has the crowd clapping along. I tap my foot to the beat, caught up in the infectious holiday spirit.

As float after float passes by, each more elaborate than the last, I watch Chad's face light up with wonder. His excitement is contagious, and I see the parade through new eyes. The bakery's gingerbread house float really is a sight to behold, the scent of fresh-baked cookies wafting from it making my mouth water.

"Look, Mom!" Chad tugs on Molly's sleeve, pointing at the hardware store's workshop float. "The elves are really moving!"

Molly leans down, her arm wrapping around Chad's shoulders. "I see them, honey. It's amazing, isn't it?"

I watch their interaction and my heavy coat has

nothing to do with why I feel so warm inside. They fit so perfectly into this scene, into this life in Benton Falls. The sight of them, framed by twinkling lights and the joyful atmosphere of the parade, is like something out of a Christmas card.

And yet...

The weight of Morgan's offer sits heavy in my pocket, a constant reminder of the choice that lies before me. I should've left it home in the drawer. The parade continues, a blur of lights and music and laughter, but I find my thoughts drifting. I imagine myself on a TV set, sharing Christmas traditions from around the world. The excitement of travel, of new experiences, of fulfilling that long-held dream of seeing what lies beyond Benton Falls...

"Evan?" Molly's voice breaks through my reverie. "Are you okay? You seem a million miles away."

I blink, focusing on her concerned face. The parade continues around us, but at this moment, it's as if the world has narrowed to just the two of us.

"I'm fine," I say automatically, but the words feel hollow. Molly's brow furrows, and I know she's not buying it. She's always been able to see right through me.

"Evan," she says as her hand squeezes mine. "What's going on? You've been... different lately. Distant."

I swallow hard, feeling the weight of the moment. This isn't how I planned to have this conversation, surrounded by the joy and excitement of the parade. But looking into Molly's eyes, seeing the mixture of concern and affection there, I know I can't keep this from her any longer.

EVAN

"Molly, I..." I start, then falter. How do I explain the turmoil in my heart? The conflict between the life I'm building here and the dreams I've held onto for so long?

Chad's excited voice cuts through the tension. "Mom! Evan! Look, it's Santa!"

Sure enough, the highlight of the parade is approaching. Santa's sleigh, pulled by "reindeer" on roller skates, glides down Main Street. Children cheer and wave, their faces alight with wonder.

But Molly's eyes never leave my face. "Evan," she says, her voice barely audible over the crowd's excitement. "Please. Talk to me."

I take a deep breath, steeling myself. "Morgan offered me a job," I blurt out, the words tumbling from me in a rush. "With her new station. Traveling, sharing Christmas traditions from around the world. It's... it's everything I used to dream about."

I see the moment my words register, the flash of hurt in Molly's eyes before she masks it. She pulls her hand from mine, and I feel the loss of contact like a physical ache.

"Oh," she says, her voice carefully neutral. "I see. And... are you going to take it?"

The parade continues around us, a stark contrast to the bubble of tension we're trapped in. Santa waves from his sleigh, children laugh and cheer, but all I can focus on is the guarded look in Molly's eyes.

"I don't know," I admit, hating the uncertainty in my voice. "I haven't decided yet. It's a big opportunity, but..."

"But what?" Molly prompts, and I can hear the strain in her voice, the effort it's taking her to remain calm.

"But I have a life here," I say, reaching for her hand again. She lets me take it, but her fingers remain limp in my grasp. "The farm, the community... you and Chad. It's not an easy decision."

Molly's eyes search my face, and I can see the conflict there, the hope warring with fear. "When were you going to tell me about this?"

I wince at the hurt in her voice. "I was going to. I just... I needed time to think it through. To figure out what I really want."

As soon as the words leave my mouth, I know they're the wrong ones. Molly pulls her hand away, taking a step back. The space between us feels vast, despite the crowd pressing in around us.

"What you really want," she repeats, her voice flat. "I see."

"Molly, that's not what I meant—"

But she cuts me off, shaking her head. "No, I think it's exactly what you meant, Evan. You needed time to decide if we—if this life here—is what you really want."

The pain in her eyes is unmistakable now, and it cuts me to the core. I've hurt her, the last thing I ever wanted to do.

"Mom?" Chad's voice breaks through our tension. He's looking between us, confusion clear on his face. "What's wrong?"

Molly forces a smile, but it doesn't reach her eyes. "Nothing, honey. We're just talking. Why don't you go see if you can catch some of the candy canes Mrs. Claus is throwing?"

Chad hesitates for a moment, his gaze flickering between us, before the lure of candy wins out. As he darts off into the crowd, Molly turns back to me.

"I think we should call it a night," she says, her voice quiet but firm. "Chad and I should head home."

"Molly, please," I say, reaching for her again. "Let's talk about this. I don't want to leave things like this."

She steps back, avoiding my touch. "I think we both need some time to think, Evan. You clearly have a lot to consider."

The finality in her tone feels like a blow to the gut. I watch helplessly as she calls Chad back, as they gather their things. The parade continues around us, but the joy and magic of the evening have evaporated, leaving only a hollow ache in my chest.

"Goodnight, Evan," Molly says, her voice barely audible over the crowd's cheers. "Merry Christmas."

Before I can respond, she's gone, leading Chad through the throng of people. I stand there, surrounded by the festive atmosphere of the parade, feeling more alone than I have in months.

The rest of the parade passes in a blur. I'm vaguely aware of Santa's sleigh making its final pass, of the crowd beginning to disperse, but it all feels distant, unreal. My mind is replaying the conversation with Molly, seeing the hurt in her eyes, the way she pulled away from me.

As I make my way back to my truck, the streets of Benton Falls seem different. The twinkling lights that had seemed so magical earlier now feel cold and distant. The laughter and chatter of families heading home grate on my nerves, a stark reminder of what I might be losing.

The drive back to the farm is silent, save for the crunch of gravel under my tires. As I pull up to the farmhouse, its dark windows a reflection of the emptiness I feel inside, I'm struck by how different everything looks. Just this morning, this place had felt full of possibility, of warmth, of the future I was building with Molly and Chad. Now, it feels like a reminder of all I stand to lose.

I make my way inside, not bothering to turn on the lights. In the darkness of the living room, I sink into my favorite armchair, the weight of the evening settling over me like a heavy blanket.

What have I done?

The question echoes in my mind as I replay the evening's events. Molly's hurt expression, the distance in her eyes as she said goodnight, the confusion on Chad's face... it all haunts me.

I pull Morgan's business card out of my pocket, staring at it in the dim light filtering through the windows. This little piece of cardstock, with its promise of adventure and new horizons, suddenly feels like a curse. Is this what I really want? To leave behind everything I've built here, the connections I've made, the love that's been growing between Molly and me?

But even as I question it, I can't deny the small thrill that runs through me at the thought of travel, of seeing the world, of fulfilling the dreams I've held onto for so

EVAN

long. It's a part of me, this wanderlust, as much as the roots I've put down in Benton Falls.

As I sit there in the darkness, I'm struck by the irony of it all. For years, I've felt tied to this place, dreaming of escape. And now that the opportunity is here, now that I have the chance to leave... I'm terrified of losing what I have.

I think back to the first day Molly and Chad came to the farm. The way her eyes lit up when she saw the wreaths and the trees. I remember Chad's excitement the first time he helped me choose a Christmas tree for a customer, his face beaming with pride.

These memories, once a source of warmth and joy, now feel tainted by the hurt I saw in Molly's eyes tonight. I stand up abruptly, unable to sit still with the weight of my thoughts. Pacing the room, I try to sort through the jumble of emotions coursing through me. Guilt, longing, fear, excitement - they all war within me, leaving me feeling raw and confused.

Part of me wants to rush to Molly's house, to explain everything, to beg for understanding. But I know that's not the answer. She was right - we both need time to think.

As I pass by the mantle, my eyes fall on a photo taken just a few weeks ago. It's of Molly, Chad, and me amongst the Christmas trees. We're all laughing, covered in pine needles, our cheeks red from the cold. We look... happy. Like a family.

The sight of it stops me in my tracks. Is this what I'm

willing to give up? This warmth, this sense of belonging, this love that's been growing between us?

But then my gaze shifts to the window, to the stars twinkling in the clear night sky. They seem to call to me, reminding me of all the places I've dreamed of seeing, all the adventures I've longed to have.

I sink back into the armchair, feeling torn in two. As the clock on the mantle chimes midnight, I'm no closer to a decision. The parade's festive atmosphere feels like a distant memory, replaced by the heavy silence of the farmhouse and the weight of the choice before me.

I close my eyes, wishing for clarity, for a sign of what I should do. But all I see is Molly's hurt expression, the disappointment in her eyes as she walked away.

What have I done? And more importantly, what am I going to do now?

The questions linger in the air, unanswered, as the night wears on. Outside, the world is blanketed in the quiet peace of a winter's night. But inside, in the darkness of the farmhouse, my heart and mind continue their tumultuous debate, leaving me feeling more lost and uncertain than ever before.

As the first light of dawn creeps through the windows, I realize I've spent the entire night in that chair, turning over every possibility in my mind. My body aches from the lack of movement, but it's nothing compared to the ache in my heart.

I stand, stretching my stiff muscles, and make my way to the kitchen. The coffee maker gurgles to life, filling the air with the rich aroma of brewing coffee. It's a comforting scent, a part of my daily routine, but today it feels hollow, just another reminder of how everything has changed.

As I wait for the coffee to brew, I stare out the window at the farm. The sun is just beginning to peek over the horizon, casting a soft golden glow over the rows of evergreens. It's a sight I've seen countless times, but today it feels different. Today, I'm seeing it through the lens of potential loss.

I think about Morgan's offer, about the excitement of travel and new experiences. But then my mind drifts back to Molly, to the hurt in her eyes last night, to the way she pulled away from me.

A new thought occurs to me, one that sends a chill through my body despite the warmth of the kitchen. What if Molly doesn't really care about me as much as I thought? If she truly cared, wouldn't she have stayed to talk it through, to understand my perspective?

The coffee maker beeps, signaling it's done, but I hardly notice. My mind is racing now, replaying every interaction with Molly, searching for signs I might have missed.

She ran away at the first sign of a problem. Just like that, she shut down and walked away. Is that how she handles all difficulties? Is that the kind of relationship I want to be in?

I pour myself a cup of coffee, the familiar action feeling strangely disconnected from reality. As I take the first sip, the bitter taste matches my mood.

Maybe I've been fooling myself all along. Maybe

what I thought was growing between us was just a comfortable illusion, a way to feel less lonely in a place I've always felt trapped.

The farm suddenly feels confining, the walls of the kitchen closing in on me. I've spent so long trying to convince myself that I could be happy here, that I could find fulfillment in this life. But what if I've just been lying to myself?

Morgan's offer floats back into my mind, no longer feeling like a temptation, but like a lifeline. A chance to break free, to see the world, to find out who I really am outside of this town and this farm.

Maybe I should take the job. Maybe this is the wake-up call I needed to realize that my dreams of travel and adventure aren't just youthful fantasies, but a core part of who I am.

As I drain the last of my coffee, a sense of resolve settles over me. I've spent too long trying to fit myself into a life that might not be right for me. It's time to take a chance, to make a decision.

I reach for my phone, my finger hovering over Morgan's number. The first rays of sunlight stream through the window, illuminating the kitchen in a soft glow. It feels like a sign, a new day dawning, full of possibilities.

With a deep breath, I press the call button. As the phone rings, I feel a mix of excitement and trepidation. Whatever happens next, I know one thing for certain: nothing will ever be the same again.

Twenty

BETTY

Benton Falls shimmers around me as I stand just outside Sweet Haven Bakery & Café. The scent of freshly baked cinnamon rolls and brewing coffee fills my senses, a stark contrast to the ethereal fragrances of the celestial realm I've just left. Through the frosted windows, I can see the warm glow of fairy lights and the sparkle of tinsel garlands. The town square is alive with last-minute Christmas shoppers, their laughter and excited chatter creating a festive atmosphere.

As I step inside the bakery, the warmth envelops me like a hug. Maggie Whitfield, the owner, is bustling behind the counter, her cheeks flushed with exertion and holiday cheer. The aroma of baked goods is even stronger inside, a heady mix of sugar, spice, and comfort that seems to embody the very essence of Christmas.

I spot Evan sitting at a corner table, his fingers drumming nervously on the worn wood surface. His blue eyes are fixed on the door, a mix of anticipation and uncertainty clear on his face. My heart aches for him, knowing the internal struggle he's facing.

Taking a deep breath, I make my way to the counter, ordering a cup of peppermint hot chocolate and one of Maggie's famous apple turnovers. As I wait for my order, I keep one eye on Evan, watching as Morgan Caldwell breezes through the door.

Morgan's entrance causes a stir in the bakery. She's dressed impeccably in a tailored red coat, her dark hair styled in perfect waves. She exudes confidence and success, and I can see Evan straighten in his chair as she approaches.

"Evan," Morgan greets him, her voice carrying across the bakery. "Merry Christmas Eve."

"Merry Christmas Eve, Morgan," Evan replies, standing to greet her. "I'm glad you could meet me."

I watch as Morgan reaches into her designer handbag, pulling out a business card. "I'm afraid I can't stay long," she says, her tone brisk but not unkind. "But I wanted to give you this. It's my boss's card. He's very interested in having you on the show."

Evan takes the card, looking slightly bewildered. "Oh, I thought we were going to discuss the details..."

Morgan shakes her head, a small smile playing on her lips. "There's nothing to discuss, Evan. Your dreams are waiting for you. All you have to do is reach out and grab them."

With that, she turns on her heel and walks out, leaving Evan standing there, the business card clutched in his hand and a look of confusion on his face.

This is my moment, I realize. The pivotal point where I can help Evan see the truth of his heart. But how?

I close my eyes, reaching out with my angelic senses as Evan takes his seat. I can feel the turmoil of emotions swirling within Evan—excitement, fear, longing, and underneath it all, a deep, aching love for Molly and Chad.

Taking a deep breath, I pick up my hot chocolate and turnover and make my way to Evan's table.

"Mind if I join you?" I ask, keeping my voice light and friendly.

Evan looks up, seeming almost relieved to see a familiar face. "Betty, hi. Of course, please sit."

As I settle into the chair across from him, I can see the business card still clutched in his hand. "That seemed like an interesting encounter," I say, nodding towards the door Morgan just exited through.

Evan sighs, running a hand through his hair. "Yeah, it was... not what I expected. I thought we were going to talk about the job offer, but she just gave me this card and left."

I take a sip of my hot chocolate, savoring the minty sweetness as I consider my next words carefully. "Maybe it's not about the job offer itself," I suggest gently. "Maybe it's about what the offer represents."

Evan looks at me quizzically. "How do you know about...wait, what do you mean?"

I set down my mug, meeting his gaze. "Well, think about it. What does that card really mean to you? Is it just a job, or is it something more?"

I can see the wheels turning in Evan's mind as he

considers my question. "I guess... it represents adventure. The chance to see the world, to break free from the responsibilities here."

I nod encouragingly. "And those are things you've always dreamed of, right?"

"Yeah," Evan says softly, his eyes distant. "For as long as I can remember, I've wanted to get out of Benton Falls, to see what else is out there."

"But dreams can change," I say gently. "Sometimes, what we think we want isn't really what our hearts truly desire."

Evan's brow furrows as he processes my words. "What are you saying, Betty?"

I lean forward, my voice soft but intense. "I'm saying that sometimes, the greatest adventures, the most fulfilling dreams, are right in front of us. We just have to look."

As I speak, I use my angelic abilities to subtly enhance the ambient sounds of the bakery. The laughter of children excitedly discussing their Christmas wishes, the warm greetings between old friends reuniting for the holidays, the gentle tinkling of the bell above the door as families come and go. All these sounds weave together, creating a tapestry of community and love that surrounds us.

I can see Evan's expression softening as he takes in the atmosphere. "It is pretty special here," he admits. "Especially at Christmas."

"It is," I agree. "And it's not just the place, Evan. It's

the people. The connections you've made, the lives you've touched."

As if on cue, Maggie appears at our table, setting down a plate with a fresh cinnamon roll. "On the house," she says with a wink. "Merry Christmas, Evan. And thank you for all you do for this community."

Evan looks genuinely touched. "Thank you, Maggie. Merry Christmas to you too."

As Maggie walks away, I can see a shift in Evan's demeanor. He's looking around the bakery with new eyes, taking in the familiar faces, the warmth, the sense of belonging.

"You know," he says slowly, "when my parents retired and I took over the farm, I saw it as a burden. Something tying me down. But lately..."

"Lately?" I prompt gently.

"Lately, it's felt different. Like it's not just a job, but a part of who I am. A way to contribute to this community, to be a part of something bigger than myself."

I nod encouragingly. "And what about Molly and Chad? How do they fit into this new perspective?"

At the mention of their names, Evan's face softens, a look of tenderness and love that takes my breath away. "They've changed everything," he says softly. "Molly, with her strength and kindness. And Chad... his enthusiasm, his joy... they've made me see the farm, see Benton Falls, in a whole new light."

"It sounds like they've become very important to you," I say.

Evan nods, his eyes distant. "They have. More than I ever thought possible. The thought of leaving them..."

He trails off, and I can see the moment of realization dawning in his eyes. It's like watching the sun break through clouds, illuminating everything in a new, clear light.

"Oh my gosh," he breathes. "What am I doing? How could I even think about leaving?"

I reach out, patting his hand gently. "Sometimes we need a little distance to see what's truly important. There's no shame in that, Evan. The important thing is that you see it now."

Evan looks at me, his eyes shining with unshed tears. "I do see it. I see it so clearly now. Everything I've ever wanted, everything I've been searching for... it's been right here all this time. In this town, on that farm, with Molly and Chad."

I feel a surge of joy and pride, knowing that I've helped Evan reach this epiphany. But I know my job isn't quite done yet.

"So, what are you going to do now?" I ask gently.

Evan stands up abruptly, a new energy radiating from him. "I need to find Molly. I need to tell her... everything. How I feel, what I want. I just hope it's not too late."

I smile, feeling the warmth of divine approval flowing through me. "It's never too late for love, Evan. Especially on Christmas Eve."

As Evan rushes out of the bakery, pausing only long enough to wish Maggie a Merry Christmas, I feel a sense of completion wash over me. I've done it. I've helped

Evan see the truth of his heart, guided him towards the love and gratitude that was always there, waiting to be discovered.

I close my eyes, ready to return to the celestial realm, and report my success to Henry. But before I can dematerialize, I feel a gentle tap on my shoulder.

I open my eyes to find Maggie standing there, a knowing smile on her face. "You know," she says, "I've seen a lot of Christmas miracles in my time, but what you just did for Evan... that was something special."

For a moment, I'm taken aback. Can she see me for what I truly am? But then I realize it doesn't matter. Angel or human, what matters is the love and kindness we show to one another.

"Thank you, Maggie," I say, my voice thick with emotion. "Merry Christmas."

Maggie's eyes twinkle with a wisdom that seems beyond her years. "Merry Christmas to you too, Betty. I'm grateful there are angels like you around."

I feel a jolt of surprise, but before I can respond, Maggie continues, "Oh, don't worry. Your secret's safe with me. I've always believed there were angels among us, especially at Christmas."

I smile, feeling a warmth spread through me at her words. "Well, Maggie, I'd say you're a bit of an angel yourself. The way you bring people together in this bakery, the love you put into everything you do... it's its own kind of miracle."

Maggie blushes, waving off my compliment. "Oh, hush. I just do what anyone would do. Now, tell me, what do you think is going to happen with Evan and Molly?"

I can't help but grin, feeling a surge of excitement. "I have a feeling that this Christmas is going to be very special for both of them. Love has a way of finding its path, especially when it's meant to be."

Maggie nods, her eyes bright with anticipation. "Well, I can't wait to see it unfold. Those two deserve all the happiness in the world."

As we chat, the bakery bustling around us with the warmth and joy of Christmas Eve, I feel a deep sense of contentment. This is what it's all about, I realize. Not grand gestures or miraculous interventions, but the small moments of connection, of kindness, of love shared between people.

As Maggie returns to her customers and I prepare to make my way back to the celestial realm, I take one last look around the bakery. The twinkling lights, the laughter of families, the aroma of freshly baked treats - it all blends together into a perfect snapshot of Christmas magic.

With a heart full of joy and excitement, I step out into the crisp winter air of Benton Falls, ready to see just what happens next. Evan's heart is in the right place—I just hope I can say the same for Molly.

Twenty-One

EVAN

The winter wind nips at my cheeks as I rush through the streets of Benton Falls, my heart pounding with a mixture of anticipation and fear. The town is alive with Christmas Eve excitement, twinkling lights adorning every lamppost and storefront, but I barely notice the festive atmosphere. My mind is focused on one thing only: Molly.

How could I have been so blind?

The realization of what I almost threw away hits me like a physical force, propelling me forward with renewed urgency. The weight of Morgan's boss's business card, still tucked in my pocket, feels like a lead weight—a reminder of the momentary lapse that nearly cost me everything that truly matters.

As I round the corner onto Molly's street, I'm struck by the sight of her modest sage-green bungalow. The small front porch is adorned with a simple wreath and twinkling white lights, a warm glow emanating from the windows. It's not grand or fancy, but it radiates a sense of home that makes my chest ache with longing.

I pause at the foot of her driveway, suddenly unsure. What if I'm too late? What if she doesn't want to hear what I have to say? The doubt threatens to overwhelm me, but then I remember Betty's words from the bakery: "It's never too late for love, Evan. Especially on Christmas Eve."

Taking a deep breath, I square my shoulders and make my way to the front door.

There's a hint of fresh snow in the air, mingling with the crisp winter breeze. I can hear the faint strains of "Silent Night" playing from inside, and for a moment, I'm transported back to all the Christmases of my childhood—the warmth, the love, the sense of belonging.

Before I can second-guess myself again, I raise my hand and knock on the door. The seconds that pass feel like an eternity, each one stretching out with agonizing slowness. And then, suddenly, the door swings open, and there she is.

Molly stands before me, her chestnut hair slightly mussed, wearing a soft green sweater that brings out the flecks of gold in her hazel eyes. For a moment, we just stare at each other, the air between us charged with unspoken emotions.

"Evan?" she says, her voice a mixture of surprise and wariness. "What are you doing here?"

I swallow hard, trying to find the right words. How do I express the tumult of emotions swirling inside me?

EVAN

How do I make her understand that in the span of a few hours, my entire world view has shifted?

"Molly, I... I made a mistake," I begin, the words tumbling out in a rush. "I've been so focused on what I thought I wanted, on this idea of adventure and freedom, that I almost missed the most incredible adventure of all — the one right here, with you and Chad."

Her expression softens slightly, but I can still see the hurt in her eyes. "Evan, I–"

"Please," I interrupt gently, "let me finish. I've been taking so much for granted—this town, the farm, the people here. But most of all, I've been taking you for granted. You and Chad... you've brought so much light into my life, so much joy. The thought of leaving, of giving that up... it's unthinkable."

I take a step closer, my heart in my throat. "I love you, Molly. I love Chad. You're not just part of my life—you are my life. And if you'll let me, I want to spend every day showing you how grateful I am for that."

Molly's eyes glisten with unshed tears, and for a moment, I'm terrified I've said too much, too soon. But then she reaches out, her hand gently cupping my cheek. The warmth of her touch sends a shiver through me, igniting a spark of hope in my chest.

"Oh, Evan," she whispers, her voice thick with emotion. "I love you too. But I'm scared. What if you wake up one day and regret staying? What if–"

I shake my head, covering her hand with mine. "That's not going to happen. I know that now. Everything I've ever wanted, everything I've been searching for

—it's right here. In this town, on that farm, with you and Chad. That's the adventure I want, Molly. That's the life I choose."

A single tear escapes, trailing down Molly's cheek. I gently wipe it away with my thumb, marveling at the softness of her skin. "I'm sorry I hurt you," I say. "I'm sorry I made you doubt for even a second how important you are to me. But if you'll give me another chance, I promise to spend the rest of my life making sure you never doubt it again."

For a moment, the world seems to hold its breath. And then, slowly, a smile breaks across Molly's face—a smile so radiant it puts all the Christmas lights in Benton Falls to shame.

"I think I can manage that," she says, her eyes twinkling with a mixture of love and mischief.

Before I can respond, a small voice pipes up from behind Molly. "Mom? Who's at the door?"

Chad appears, his sandy hair tousled and his eyes wide with curiosity. When he sees me, his face lights up. "Evan! Are you here to help us hang up our stockings? Mom said we had to wait until Christmas Eve, and it's finally Christmas Eve!"

I look at Molly, silently asking permission. She nods, her smile soft and welcoming. "I think that sounds like a wonderful idea," she says. "What do you say, Evan? Want to help us hang up stockings?"

My heart swells with emotion. This—this right here —is everything I've ever wanted. "I'd love nothing more," I say, my voice rough with feeling.

EVAN

As I step into the warmth of Molly's home, I'm enveloped by the scent of pine and freshly baked cookies. The living room is cozy and inviting, with mismatched furniture that somehow fits perfectly together. The tree is all aglow and flames dance in the hearth.

Chad immediately grabs my hand, pulling me towards a box of ornaments. "Come on, Evan! I want to show you the ornament I made at school. It's a reindeer, but I used pinecones for the body instead of wood slices!"

I laugh, allowing myself to be led by his enthusiasm. "That sounds amazing, buddy. I can't wait to see it."

As he points to the ornament on the tree, I'm struck by the simple joy of the moment. Chad's excitement is infectious, his laughter filling the room as he tells me about each ornament.

Molly walks over with stockings draped over her arm. She hands one to Chad and one to me. "I hope you don't mind," Molly says as I hold the stocking, running my fingers over my name stitched across the top. "I got this for you. I guess I was hoping you'd be spending Christmas Eve with us."

I'm overwhelmed by the thoughtfulness of the gesture. "Molly, I... thank you. This means more than you know."

She smiles, reaching out to squeeze my hand. "Every family member needs a stocking."

Family. The word echoes in my mind, filling me with a warmth that spreads from my core to the tips of my fingers. Is that what we are? What we could be?

As if reading my thoughts, Chad pipes up, "Does this

mean you're going to be here for Christmas morning too, Evan? Because that would be the best present ever!"

I look at Molly, not wanting to overstep. She meets my gaze, her eyes soft with love and invitation. "What do you say, Evan? Want to join us for Christmas morning?"

My heart feels like it might burst with happiness. "I'd love nothing more," I say, my voice thick with emotion.

Chad lets out a whoop of joy, launching himself at me for a hug. I catch him, lifting him up and spinning him around as his laughter fills the room. When I set him down, I find Molly watching us, her eyes shining with unshed tears of happiness.

I reach out, pulling her into our embrace. For a moment, we stand there, the three of us wrapped in each other's arms, the twinkling lights of the Christmas tree casting a warm glow over us. This, I realize, is what home feels like. This is what love feels like.

As we pull apart, I'm struck by a sudden thought. "You know," I say, "there's still one Christmas tradition we haven't covered yet."

Molly raises an eyebrow, a smile playing at the corners of her mouth. "Oh? And what's that?"

I grin, feeling a surge of excitement. "The church's candlelight service. It's not Christmas Eve without it. What do you say we bundle up and head down to the church?"

Chad's eyes light up. "Can we, Mom? Please?"

Molly pretends to consider for a moment, but I can see the answer in her eyes before she speaks. "Well, I suppose we can't break tradition, can we? Let's do it."

The next few minutes are a flurry of activity as we bundle up in coats, scarves, and mittens. As we step out into the cool night air, I'm struck by the beauty of Benton Falls on Christmas Eve. The streets are lined with luminarias, their soft glow creating a path of light through the town. The sound of carols drifts on the breeze, growing stronger as we near the town square.

Chad walks between us, his small hand in mine, chattering excitedly about the service and wondering if we'll see any of his school friends there. Molly walks on his other side, her arm linked through mine, her presence a warm comfort in the cold night.

As we reach the church, I'm overwhelmed by the sight before us. The old colonial building stands proudly against the night sky, its windows aglow with warm light. People are filing in, their faces bright with anticipation and joy. The air is filled with the scent of pine from the wreaths adorning the doors and the sound of greetings exchanged between friends and neighbors.

We find seats near the back of the church, and I'm handed three candles by a smiling usher. As we wait for the service to begin, I look around at the faces of my neighbors, my friends, my community. I see joy, love, hope—all the things that make this season so special.

The pastor steps forward, his voice ringing out across the sanctuary as he welcomes everyone to the service. As he speaks about the spirit of Christmas, about love and togetherness, I feel Molly lean into me, her head resting on my shoulder.

"Thank you," she whispers, her voice barely audible over the pastor's words.

I look down at her, confused. "For what?"

She smiles, her eyes reflecting the candlelight. "For coming back. For choosing us. For making this the best Christmas Eve I can remember."

My heart swells with emotion. "No, Molly. Thank you. For showing me what really matters. For helping me see the beauty in the life I have. I'm the lucky one here."

As the first notes of "Silent Night" begin to play, we light our candles, the flame passing from person to person until the entire church is aglow. Chad stands in front of us, his face a picture of wonder as he carefully holds his candle, singing along with all the enthusiasm of a nine-year-old boy.

I wrap my arm around Molly's waist, pulling her close as we join in the singing. In this moment, surrounded by the warmth of community and the love of this incredible woman and her son, I'm overwhelmed by a sense of gratitude so profound it brings tears to my eyes.

This is what I've been searching for all along. Not some far-off adventure or grand dream, but this: the simple joy of being part of something larger than myself. Of having a place to belong, people to love, a community to serve.

As the final notes of the carol fade away, I turn to Molly. The candlelight flickers across her face, highlighting the softness of her features, the warmth in her eyes. Without a word, I lean in, my lips meeting hers in a kiss that feels like coming home.

It's soft and sweet, filled with promise and love and the magic of Christmas. When we part, I rest my forehead against hers, savoring the moment.

"I love you, Molly Bennett," I whisper, my voice rough with emotion. "You and Chad... you're my home, my adventure, my everything."

She smiles, her eyes shining with happy tears. "And we love you, Evan Lawson. Merry Christmas."

The service concludes, and we file out of the church, the cool night air a refreshing contrast to the warmth inside. Chad skips ahead, his energy seemingly boundless even at this late hour.

"Can we go see the big tree in the square?" he asks, his eyes bright with excitement.

I look at Molly, who nods with a smile. "Of course we can, buddy," I say, ruffling his hair. "Lead the way."

Hand in hand, the three of us make our way through the quiet streets towards the town square. The massive Christmas tree stands tall and proud, its lights twinkling like stars in the night sky. As we approach, I hear the faint chiming of the courthouse clock.

"It's almost midnight," Molly says, her breath visible in the cold air.

We stand there, gazing up at the tree, as the clock begins to strike. With each chime, I feel a wave of gratitude wash over me.

For this town.

For this moment.

For the love I've found.

As the twelfth strike fades away, heralding the arrival of Christmas Day, I pull Molly and Chad close. The square is quiet, peaceful, bathed in the soft glow of the Christmas lights.

"Merry Christmas," I whisper, my voice thick with emotion.

"Merry Christmas, Evan," Molly replies, her eyes shining with love.

"Merry Christmas!" Chad echoes, his excitement palpable even through his sleepiness.

As we stand there, wrapped in each other's arms beneath the twinkling lights of the town square Christmas tree, I'm filled with a sense of peace and rightness that I've never known before. The restlessness that has plagued me for so long has been replaced by a deep, abiding gratitude.

When the bells fade into the night and the first minutes of Christmas Day tick by, I send up a silent prayer of thanks. For second chances, for open hearts, and for the magic of Christmas that brought me home in every sense of the word.

This, I realize, is the greatest adventure of all. And I'm grateful—so incredibly grateful—for every step of the journey that led me here.

BETTY

The celestial hall shimmers with a soft, golden light as I stand before the grand lecturn. The vastness of the space is awe-inspiring, its marble floors cool beneath my feet and its atmosphere charged with divine energy. Despite the room's capacity to hold countless angels, today only two occupy the front row: my mentor, Henry, his kind eyes twinkling with encouragement, and the imposing figure of Saint Nicholas, his silvery beard catching the ethereal light.

My heart, though no longer beating in the earthly sense, seems to flutter with a mixture of excitement and nervousness. This is it—the moment I've been working towards since I first embarked on my journey as a guardian angel in training. The culmination of my assignment with Evan, Molly, and Chad in the picturesque town of Benton Falls.

I take a deep breath, more out of habit than necessity, and begin.

"Esteemed mentors, Henry and Saint Nicholas, I stand before you today not just as Betty, the guardian angel in training, but as a soul transformed by the very lesson I was tasked to teach."

My voice, imbued with a confidence I never possessed in life, rings out clear and strong in the grand hall. As I speak, I notice a soft golden glow beginning to emanate from my form, a majestic manifestation of the joy and purpose I feel.

"When I was first assigned to guide Evan Lawson towards a path of gratitude, I must confess I felt woefully unprepared. How could I, who had experienced such hardship and loneliness in my earthly life, possibly teach another the value of being thankful?"

I pause, remembering those first uncertain days in Benton Falls. The scent of pine and cinnamon seems to waft through the hall, a sensory reminder of the Christmas tree farm that became the backdrop for our story.

"But as I watched Evan struggle with his own discontent, as I witnessed the blossoming love between him and Molly, and as I saw the world through young Chad's eyes, I understood. Gratitude isn't about having a perfect life. It's about recognizing the beauty in the life we have and for the blessings we've yet to receive."

I can see Henry nodding encouragingly, his eyes shining with pride. Saint Nicholas leans forward slightly, his piercing blue eyes fixed intently on me.

"Through Evan's journey, I learned that gratitude is a choice we make every day. It's in the small moments - the laughter shared over a cup of hot cocoa, the warmth of a hand held on a cold winter's night, the joy of a child's wonder at the first snowfall. These are the threads that weave the tapestry of a life well-lived, a life filled with love and purpose."

As I speak, I feel a surge of divine energy coursing through me. The golden glow around me intensifies, casting dancing shadows on the marble floor.

"But perhaps the most profound lesson I learned was about the transformative power of empathy and understanding. By truly seeing Evan, by understanding his fears and his dreams, I was able to guide him towards the gratitude that had always been within his reach."

I pause, allowing the weight of my words to settle in the room. The air seems to shimmer with celestial energy, responding to the truth of my testimony.

"In helping Evan find gratitude, I discovered my own. I found myself grateful for the very struggles that had once seemed so insurmountable in my earthly life. For it was those challenges that prepared me for this divine purpose."

I glance down at my hands, remembering the countless hours spent fumbling with heavenly fabric, trying to master the art of robe-making.

"I may never be proficient in creating celestial robes," I admit with a small chuckle, eliciting a warm smile from Henry, "but I've learned that our perceived weaknesses often lead us to our greatest strengths. My struggles with sewing taught me patience and perseverance - qualities that proved invaluable in my guardianship of Evan."

Saint Nicholas nods approvingly, his powerful presence radiating warmth and understanding.

"Gratitude," I continue, my voice swelling with emotion, "is not just a feeling. It's a force—a divine energy that has the power to transform lives, to heal hearts, to bridge the gap between heaven and earth. It's the key that unlocks the door to true joy and fulfillment."

As I speak these words, the hall seems to come alive with celestial light. Tiny sparkles of divine energy dance in the air, reminiscent of the twinkling Christmas lights that adorned Benton Falls.

"And it is with a heart full of gratitude that I look forward to continuing this heavenly work, to touching more lives, to spreading the transformative power of thankfulness."

As I conclude my speech, the air seems to vibrate with celestial energy, and for a moment, I feel connected to every soul I've ever touched, every life I've had the privilege to be a part of.

Henry is rising to his feet with tears glistening in his eyes. "Oh, Betty," he says, his voice thick with emotion, "you've done it. You've truly understood the essence of what it means to be a guardian angel."

Saint Nicholas stands as well, his imposing figure softened by the gentle smile on his face. "Well done, faithful servant," he booms, his voice like distant thunder. "You have not only completed your assignment but have embodied the very virtues you were tasked to instill."

I feel a surge of joy so intense that the golden glow

around me brightens, casting the entire hall in a warm, ethereal light. Henry approaches the Lecturn, his eyes twinkling with pride and affection.

"Betty," he says solemnly as he pulls a beautiful golden bell from his robe and rings it softly. "It is my great honor and privilege to bestow upon you your wings. You have earned them not just through your successful guidance of Evan, but through your own growth and transformation."

As Henry speaks these words, I feel a tingling sensation between my shoulder blades. A warmth spreads across my back, and suddenly, with a soft whoosh, a pair of magnificent wings unfurls behind me. They're not physical in the earthly sense, but an extension of my celestial energy—shimmering, translucent appendages that seem to be woven from strands of pure light.

The feeling is indescribable - a sense of completeness, of coming into my full divine purpose. Tears of joy stream down my face as I flex my new wings, feeling the power and responsibility they represent.

"Remember, Betty," Saint Nicholas says, his voice gentle yet powerful, "these wings are not just a symbol of your achievement, but a tool for your continued service. Use them wisely, with compassion and understanding, to lift others as you have been lifted."

I nod solemnly, feeling the weight of this new responsibility settling on my shoulders alongside the wondrous lightness of my wings. "I will," I promise, my voice steady and sure. "I will use this gift to continue spreading love, understanding, and gratitude wherever I'm called to serve."

In this moment, standing in the celestial hall with my new wings and the warmth of divine approval surrounding me, I feel a profound sense of gratitude. Gratitude for the journey, for the lessons learned, for the lives touched, and for the eternal purpose I've found.

"Thank you," I say simply, pouring all my love and appreciation into those two words.

Henry steps forward, enveloping me in a warm embrace. "No, Betty," he says softly, "thank you. For reminding us all of the transformative power of gratitude and love."

As we part, I see Saint Nicholas nodding approvingly. "Go forth, Betty," he says, his voice ringing with authority and warmth. "Go forth and continue to spread the magic of Christmas, the power of gratitude, and the transformative force of love. Your journey as a guardian angel has only just begun."

With these words, I feel a surge of excitement for what lies ahead. New assignments, new souls to guide, new opportunities to spread the lessons I've learned. But even as I look forward to the future, I cast a fond thought back to Benton Falls, to Evan, Molly, and Chad.

In my mind's eye, I see them gathered around their Christmas tree, their faces aglow with love and contentment. Evan, his arm around Molly, looking at her with a gratitude that radiates from his very being. Molly, her eyes shining with the joy of finding love and renewed hope. And Chad, his face alight with the pure wonder of childhood, reminding them all of the magic that exists in every moment.

As this vision fades, replaced by the shimmering reality of the celestial hall, I feel a sense of completion. My first assignment may be over, but the impact of it—on Evan's life, on my own journey, and on the tapestry of divine love that connects us all—will resonate for eternity.

Angel Institute Book 7

The classroom buzzes with an energy that's part nervousness, part excitement. I can't help but fidget in my cloud-like chair, my fingers drumming a silent rhythm on the polished wooden desk before me. Angel Institute is a revered school for angels in training. All sorts come here—to be honest, I didn't think they'd let me in, but admissions angels in heaven are way nicer than admissions directors on Earth. Here, they think I have potential.

I agree with them. There's something great inside of me; I just never figured out how to get it out.

Hopefully, being a guardian angel will make that happen. Maybe this is my eternal calling, and I'll finally be able to get my wings.

I breathe in deeply, savoring the crisp, clean scent of heaven—a blend of fresh-cut grass, spring flowers, and sugar doughnuts that never fails to invigorate me.

Around me, my fellow angels-in-training shift in

their seats. We've been through so much together, countless study sessions and practice missions. I glance at John, who's nervously adjusting his socks again. Poor guy looks like he's about to face judgment day instead of getting an assignment. I flash him a reassuring grin, hoping to ease some of his tension.

My attention snaps to the front of the room as Henry adjusts his glasses. "Welcome, my dear trainees," he begins, his voice warm and rich like honey. His blue eyes twinkle, and his silver hair seems even more disheveled than usual. He's been a guardian angel for ages. I wonder if he remembers what it was like to sit at these desks.

"Today is a big day. Each of you will receive a letter with your final assignment on Earth. I should tell you that you'll be going down during the Christmas season."

A ripple of excitement passes through the room. I lean forward, eager to hear more. Christmas on Earth? Count me in. Everything about this holiday says: Will. I don't know if I'll ever grow out of the sense of wonder and awe—not to mention the fun of buying gifts and keeping them secret until the 25th. I'll get to be right in the middle of it all. I hope my assignment is ready for a great time. We're going to have so much fun together. I can see us sledding, ice skating, skiing, and all of it.

Henry continues, his expression growing more serious. "Your assignments are crucial. The humans you'll be guiding are in danger of losing their Christmas spirit forever."

My eyebrows shoot up. Losing Christmas spirit? That sounds serious. But also... kind of exciting? I mean, what better challenge for a guardian angel in training than to save someone's Christmas spirit? Oh man, this is going to be awesome. I am going to rock this assignment. We'll be best friends, and he or she will forever remember my name and tell stories about me every Christmas—the angel who saved his or her Christmas spirit. I can see it all now.

"That means–" Lillian starts to say, but Henry cuts her off gently.

"It means that you are important in The Plan." His gaze sweeps across the room, meeting each of our eyes in turn. When he looks at me, I sit up straighter, puffing out my chest a bit. "Never forget that."

I nod firmly. Of course, we're important. We're guardian angels (in training), and I, for one, am ready to knock this assignment out of the park. Not to mention, I could inspire a Christmas movie that would entertain families for years to come. A Christmas classic. How great will that be?

Henry's voice pulls me back from my thoughts. "You have until midnight on Christmas Eve to fulfill your mission, and then you'll return here to give a dissertation on your experience. Pass, and you'll earn your wings. Fail, and you'll have to wait a hundred years before you can apply to try again."

A collective groan ripples through the classroom. A hundred years? The thought of waiting that long makes my stomach do a little flip.

John raises his hand, his face a mask of worry. "Is failure... possible?"

I resist the urge to roll my eyes. Of course, it's possible, John. Why else would Henry mention it? I keep my mouth shut.

Henry's lips twist in a thoughtful expression. "We have a twenty percent failure rate. It happens. But the second time around seems to be the charm, so don't be discouraged and don't worry about what happens next. Focus on the good. Work in faith. You'll do just fine."

I nod along with Henry's words, feeling a surge of confidence. Twenty percent? Those are great odds. I've always been a quick learner, always eager to take on new challenges. This assignment? It's going to be a breeze.

As Henry begins to hand out the letters, I find myself tuning out a bit. My mind is already racing ahead, imagining all the ways I could help my assignment. Maybe they need a push to reconnect with old friends. Or perhaps they've forgotten the joy of giving? Whatever it is, I'm sure I can handle it.

I'm so lost in my daydreams that I almost miss it when Henry reaches me. His eyes soften as he places the letter in my hand, giving my shoulder a gentle squeeze.

"Will," he says, his voice warm with affection, "Remember, your strength lies in your enthusiasm and your ability to connect with others. Trust yourself and what you've learned."

I beam up at him. "Thanks, Henry. I won't let you down."

As Henry moves on, I turn the letter over in my

hands. The parchment feels weighty and important. I take a deep breath, savoring the moment, then tear it open with gusto.

My eyes scan the elegant script, drinking in every word. "Assignment: Noah Montgomery, who needs to learn the spirit of self-worth."

A grin spreads across my face. Self-worth? Now, that's something I can get behind. I've always been the one pushing for more excitement in our training sessions. This Noah Montgomery won't know what hit him.

Around me, my fellow trainees are reacting to their own assignments. Rebecca sighs dramatically while Lillian grins at the prospect of guiding lost souls. Gladys giggles, and John... well, John looks like he might faint. He makes several notes on his pad of paper.

Henry wraps up with a final piece of advice, and I tune back in. "Remember, you are not alone."

We nod and rise from our seats, the air thrumming with anticipation. As we file out of the classroom, I can't help but bounce on my toes. This is it. This is my chance to prove myself, to earn my wings, to make a real difference.

Campus stretches out before us, a riot of colors and scents that always takes my breath away intermingled between the buildings. For once, I'm not tempted to linger. Earth is waiting. Noah is waiting.

I close my eyes, focusing on my destination. When I open my eyes again, I'm standing on solid ground.

I look around, taking in my surroundings. I'm in a small town, quaint and picturesque, dusted with a layer of snow. Christmas decorations adorn the storefronts and streetlamps, twinkling merrily in the early evening light. The scent of pine and cinnamon hangs in the air, mingling with the sharp tang of wood smoke.

A few people hurry past, bundled up against the cold, their breaths puffing out in little clouds. None of them notice me, of course. To them, I'm just another face in the crowd, another person out enjoying the holiday atmosphere.

I spot a sign that reads "Benton Falls Ice Rink" and feel a pull in that direction. That must be where I'll find Noah. I set off down the street, my steps light and bouncy. I can't help but grin as I go, drinking in every sight and sound.

As I approach the ice rink, I catch sight of a trailer parked nearby with a sign that reads "Ice Skate Rentals." A man stands behind the windows, his posture relaxed but somehow... resigned? He has tousled black hair and warm brown eyes, and there's a kind of quiet strength about him. This must be Noah.

I hang back for a moment, observing. Noah helps a young couple with their skate rentals; his movements are efficient but not rushed. He offers them a small smile as they leave, but it doesn't quite reach his eyes. As soon as they're gone, his shoulders slump, and he lets out a soft sigh.

My heart goes out to him. He looks... stuck. Like he's going through the motions of life without really living it.

Well, that's about to change.

I feel a surge of determination. This is going to be

amazing. Noah Montgomery, prepare yourself. Your guardian angel has arrived.

To continue reading, grab book 7 in The Angel Institute Christmas Series.

The angels in training are waiting for you!
Enjoy all the Christmas stories that fill your heart with holiday joy.

Book Club Questions

Hello, fellow readers!

We're excited you've chosen *Angel Institute: Your Assignment: Evan* for your book club. Now that you've journeyed through Evan's struggles as he learns more about gratitude this Christmas, it's time to dive deeper into the heart of the story.

These questions are designed to get you thinking about the bigger picture—the themes, character arcs, and those "aha!" moments that made the story come alive.

Whether you're pondering the challenges faced by our guardian angels in training or dissecting the complexities of human nature, we hope these questions will enrich your reading experience and lead to some enlightening discussions.

So grab your favorite beverage, settle in with your book club, and let's explore the heavenly and earthly realms of Angel Institute together. Happy discussing!

- How does Evan's initial restlessness and desire to leave Benton Falls reflect broader themes of contentment versus ambition in modern society?
- In what ways does the Christmas tree farm serve as a metaphor for Evan's personal growth throughout the story?
- How does the author use the contrast between small-town life and big-city opportunities to explore the concept of "home"?

- Discuss the role of gratitude in the story. How does Evan's perspective on his life in Benton Falls change as he learns to be more grateful?
- How does Betty's character challenge or reinforce traditional notions of guardian angels? What does her presence add to the narrative?
- Examine the relationship between Evan and Molly. How does their romance reflect larger themes of love, trust, and personal growth?
- How does Chad's character influence Evan's journey? What does his presence represent in terms of Evan's personal development?
- Discuss the symbolism of the gingerbread house contest. How does it relate to Evan's internal conflict and the larger themes of the book?

BOOK CLUB QUESTIONS

- How does the author use the changing seasons and holiday traditions to mirror Evan's emotional journey?
- Explore the theme of community in the book. How does Benton Falls as a whole contribute to Evan's transformation?
- How does Morgan's job offer serve as a catalyst for Evan's self-discovery? What does it represent in terms of his personal goals and fears?
- Discuss the role of family legacy in the story. How does Evan's relationship with the farm evolve throughout the narrative?
- How does the author use dreams and visions to explore Evan's subconscious desires and fears?
- Examine the theme of second chances in the book. How do various characters, including Evan and Molly, embrace or struggle with the concept?
- How does Betty's own journey as a guardian angel in training parallel Evan's story? What lessons do they both learn about gratitude and purpose?
- Discuss the epilogue from Betty's perspective. How does it tie together the themes of the book, and what message does it leave readers with about gratitude, love, and personal growth?

Acknowledgments

Writing a book is never a solitary endeavor, and we are profoundly grateful for the incredible team of individuals who have supported us throughout this journey.

First and foremost, we want to express our heartfelt thanks to our amazing beta readers: Rolayne, Marissa, and Renee. Your keen insights, thoughtful feedback, and unwavering enthusiasm have been invaluable. You truly are the best beta readers we could have hoped for, and this series is better because of your contributions.

A special thank you goes to Richard for his meticulous consistency read. Your eagle eye for detail and ability to catch those elusive inconsistencies that somehow slip through have been instrumental in polishing our work to a shine.

We are deeply appreciative of Shaylee for her unwavering support and for helping us launch the Angels Unscripted podcast. Your creativity and dedication have opened up new avenues for us to connect with our readers and share the world of the Angel Institute.

To our wonderful reviewers, we cannot thank you enough. Your thoughtful words and enthusiasm for our books have been a constant source of motivation. Your efforts in spreading the word about the Angel Institute series have been crucial in helping us reach new readers. We are truly grateful for your support and advocacy.

Lastly, to our readers – thank you for embarking on this heavenly adventure with us. Your love for our characters and stories makes all the late nights and rewrites worthwhile.

This series is a labor of love, made possible by the collective efforts of many. We are blessed to have such an incredible community surrounding us, and we thank you all from the bottom of our hearts.

Also by Erica Penrod

Billionaire Bachelor Cove Series

Cowboy Reality Romance Series

Heaven and A Cowboy Series

My Heart Channel Romance Series

Country Brides Cowboy Boots Series

Mountain Cove Series

Billionaire Academy Series

The Lone Horse Ranch

Snowed In For Christmas Series

Diamond Cove Romantic Comedy Series

By E.B Penrod

Ever Eden

About the Author

Erica is a romance-loving storyteller, a certified organizer, and Diet Pepsi enthusiast, who has written over 25 contemporary romance novels. Inspired by her family's rodeo lifestyle, her stories often feature galloping horses and wild romance. But that's not all! When she's not penning heart-fluttering tales, Erica transforms into E.B. Penrod, crafting enchanting romantasy novels. Whether you're in the mood for a swoon-worthy love story or something with a supernatural twist, Erica's got you covered.

Milton Keynes UK
Ingram Content Group UK Ltd.
UKHW031619231124
451036UK00004B/42